The Amber Cat

"Do you believe in them?" asked Robin.

"Ghosts?"

"Yes," said Robin.

"Yes," his mother replied, and laughed at his startled face. "Not Sun Dance's kind, but I do believe there are occasionally people who stray from their own time into another."

"What for?" asked Robin.

"I don't know," said his mother. "Company perhaps. Curiosity. Why would anyone? Why would you?"

"I wouldn't," said Robin, "unless I had friends there."

"Perhaps they have friends there," said Mrs Brogan and she and Robin started thoughtfully into the fire for a while.

The Amber Cat

Hilary McKay

Collins
An imprint of HarperCollins*Publishers*

First published in Great Britain by Victor Gollancz 1995
First published by Collins 1997
7 9 10 8 6

Collins is an imprint of HarperCollins*Publishers* Ltd,
77-85 Fulham Palace Road, Hammersmith, London W6 8JB.

Copyright © Hilary McKay 1995

ISBN 0 00 675124-5

The author asserts the moral right to be
identified as the author of this work.

Printed and bound in Great Britain by
Caledonian International Book Manufacturing Ltd,
Glasgow, G64

To Chris Kloet
with very many thanks

CHAPTER ONE

There was chicken-pox going round the school.

"Chicken-pox in December!" groaned Robin Brogan's mother. "As if December wasn't bad enough!"

"I'm terribly sorry!" said Robin, who caught it straight away.

"Terribly?" asked his mother sceptically.

"Well, quite sorry, anyway," said Robin. "Slightly sorry. But it's got me out of the Christmas play and I feel all right except for my head. I thought chicken-pox would feel much worse than this."

"It will," said Mrs Brogan, with the gloom of one who has to do the nursing. "You always have things badly. What were you going to be in the Christmas play?"

"A beastly hobbit," said Robin, "and I'd rather have third degree chicken-pox any day!"

"All very well for you!" said Mrs Brogan (who had a quick temper but a kind heart), "but if there's one thing that I can't bear, it's poorly people kicking around the house. Getting under my feet with their spots and their sore throats. In and out of bed all day and not eating proper meals."

Robin, who heard these ungracious remarks

every time he sneezed, grinned.

"Groaning and moaning and staring out of windows..."

Robin made up his mind to put up with chicken-pox as quietly and heroically as possible.

"I'm sure they enjoy it!" said his mother. "And you ought to be in bed, not sitting there hugging that dog!"

"Why not? Might he catch chicken-pox?" asked Robin looking anxiously at Friday for signs of illness.

"I was thinking of you, not Friday," replied his mother. "He's been on the beach all afternoon and he's still very damp."

"Well, if he does catch chicken-pox at least I'll be off school to look after him," said Robin.

"Dogs don't catch chicken-pox," replied Mrs Brogan. "Thank goodness! I should be outnumbered! And I couldn't bear two lots of chicken-pox chicken-poxing about the house together!"

But, as always, her bark was worse than her bite. When the news came that Robin's best friend Dan had chicken-pox too, Mrs Brogan very nobly suggested that he come to Porridge Hall and have them there, partly as company for Robin and partly so that Dan's mother could get back to work. There was room at Porridge Hall for a school full of chicken-pox, Mrs Brogan remarked to Dan's mother.

"Heaven forbid!" she replied.

"And it would cheer up Robin," said Mrs Brogan. "We rattle around a bit, when there's only the two of us."

"You must," agreed Dan's mother, who would have hated to live at Porridge Hall. It was a big old house on the Yorkshire coast, overlooking the sea, and she could never understand why Robin's mother, usually so sensible, loved it so much. In the past it had been one house but now it was divided down the middle to make homes for two families. All through the summer and autumn the Brogan half had been full of bed and breakfasters.

("What a way to make your living!" Robin's mother often groaned, although she groaned worse when nobody came and it looked as if no living was going to be made at all.)

Now in December, Porridge Hall held only its usual people, Robin and his mother in their half, and the Robinson family who lived next door. Dan's arrival went a long way towards stopping the rattling around in the Brogan part. Friday, Robin's dog, went mad with delight, and Robin and Dan began to get better immediately, such is the power of friendship. Robin and Dan had been very good friends ever since the summer holidays, and for years before that they had been excellent enemies, so they knew and understood each other very well. Dan, who had no dog, shared Robin's and Robin, who had no father, shared Dan's. They also shared the several miles of beach opposite Porridge Hall, very many private jokes and Sun Dance, who lived next door.

Sun Dance was a nine-year-old mystery to his friends and relations. His name lingered from the days when Perry and Ant, his eleven-year-old twin brother and sister, had played at being Butch and Cassidy and had allowed him to join in as the Sun Dance Kid. The name suited him so well that it stuck; it was years since anyone had called him anything else.

"Something went wrong with the names in our family," remarked Mrs Robinson. The twins had been christened Peregrine and Antoinette after their grandparents but had sensibly shortened these romantic but frightful names, "As soon as they could speak," admitted their mother.

The youngest of the Robinson family had been named Elizabeth.

"A nice plain name," said Mrs Robinson, who by this time was beginning to learn. "Not that it made any difference."

"When I grow up," announced Elizabeth at the age of three, "I shall be a bean. A bean in a pod."

"We should have called you Beany," said Ant.

"Oh no, we shouldn't!" said Mrs Robinson, but already it was too late and four years later, even at school, they called her Beany.

The Robinson children owned a dog. Fat, beloved, scruffy and smelly, he was known as Old Blanket.

"I am tired of explaining the names in our family," said Mrs Robinson. "People must take us as they find us!"

"They are perfect names," said Robin's mother. Mrs Brogan and Mrs Robinson were best friends.

"I shall have chicken-pox too," announced Sun Dance when he heard the news from next door. "Especially if Dan is there." Sun Dance, although two years younger than Robin and Dan, adored Robin and considered he had once saved Dan's life and would have endured far worse than chicken-pox than be left out of anything they did.

"Let's all have it," suggested Robin cheerfully.

"You can't have chicken-pox twice," said Mrs Robinson when she heard this bright idea. "You four had it all together that dreadful Christmas when we kept getting power cuts. I haven't forgotten, if you have! Never again!"

However, the Robinson children were not ones to give up hope easily. School was becoming tedious. Robin was not the only one destined to be a hobbit in the school play; Perry and Ant were threatened with a similar fate, and chicken-pox, they remembered, had been most enjoyable, what with candle-lit bedrooms and unlimited ice-cream. Perry paid a secret visit to Robin and Dan next door.

"Four dirty jumpers?" repeated Robin in astonishment, on hearing Perry's request.

"What do you want to borrow four dirty jumpers for?" asked Dan.

"I'd better not tell you," said Perry virtuously.

"Oh," said Robin, as understanding suddenly dawned. "Well, anyway, I haven't got four dirty jumpers. I haven't got any at all, I don't think."

"What about the one you're wearing?" said Perry. "And Dan's? That's two!"

Robin and Dan looked doubtfully at each other.

"How would *you* like to be a hobbit?" asked Perry.

"Oh all right!" said Robin. "Come on, Dan!"

But Dan was already pulling off his jumper. Chicken-pox had arrived just in time to save him from a terrible fate. For a few horrifying days he had been cast as a singing dwarf and he knew what Perry felt like.

"It isn't fair!" said Beany, happening to notice what the twins were wearing in bed that night.

"You can have one tomorrow if you like," Perry told her.

"You'll have used up all the germs by then!

Mrs Brogan *needs* me to get chicken-pox. I could help with her bed and breakfasters."

"She hasn't got any. There's nobody staying there but Dan."

"I could help her get some, then."

"I borrowed them and it was Ant's idea so you'll just have to wait," said Perry heartlessly. Ant, however, was more sympathetic and when she woke up in the middle of the night, stifled from the effects of Dan's Aran jumper, she thoughtfully roused Beany and handed it over.

"It must be stiff with germs," she whispered happily. "It's worked on me already. I'm sure I've got a temperature."

There was great disappointment the next morning when the three jumper-wearers awoke perfectly healthy. The disappointment was made much worse when Sun Dance appeared. His chest and stomach were covered with spots and he was extremely pleased with himself.

"I bet they wash off!" said Beany, who had contemplated felt-tipping a rash on herself, but the spots did not wash off.

"However did you do it?" asked Ant.

"Easy," replied Sun Dance. "I just said, 'Please God give me chicken-pox' before I went to sleep."

"Please God give me chicken-pox," repeated Beany immediately, and gazed hopefully at her stomach.

"Really, Beany!" exclaimed Mrs Robinson. "Sun Dance, get back into bed! Beany, get ready for school!"

"It's *not* fair!" wailed Beany. "After I slept all night in Dan's smelly jumper! And I bet they're only flea-bites from Old Blanket!"

"Old Blanket hasn't got fleas," said Sun Dance.

"Oh yes he has," said Beany. "He got them from that hedgehog that died under the shed and they've been living behind his ears ever since!"

"WELL, YOU MIGHT HAVE TOLD ME BEFORE!" exclaimed her outraged mother, and she remained outraged until Perry and Beany and Ant had been packed off to school and Sun Dance had been hauled to the doctor's.

"Chicken-pox!" announced the doctor. "Yes, definitely."

"He's had them once," protested Mrs Robinson.

"Jolly well done!" said the doctor to Sun Dance and Sun Dance smirked. He did not feel the least bit ill but his spots were undeniable. As soon as he could, he showed them to Mrs Brogan next door and asked if he did not qualify as a chicken-poxer and she very kindly agreed that he did.

"Come and join the chicken-pox club at once!" she said, shooing him into the living room. "You're just what it needs! It can't be bothered to read and it hates day-time television. It sits beside the fire all day and dreams of school! It's bored!"

"We're not!" protested Robin and Dan, but all the same they were very glad to see Sun Dance, having guiltily spent the day wondering if their jumpers had been as infectious as Perry had hoped.

"Where are the others?" asked Robin.

"School," replied Sun Dance with satisfaction. "And Mum's doing Old Blanket with flea powder. Beany will be fed up, she was keeping those fleas for your mother. She thought they'd be useful for horrible bed and breakfasters. To put in their beds. To get rid of them."

"Good grief!" exclaimed Robin.

"What have you been doing?" asked Dan. "Have we missed anything? Has anything exciting happened?"

"No," said Sun Dance.

"Not even ghosts?" asked Robin, because Sun Dance was famous for seeing ghosts and always very pleased to describe them to his friends.

"Oh well, there's always ghosts," said Sun Dance. "More than ever, lately."

"It's the time of year," agreed Mrs Brogan, coming in to join them. "December is perfect for ghost stories!"

"My ghosts aren't stories," said Sun Dance, and it was true that his ghosts were certainly not at all like the ones that appeared in books.

"Tell us about them," suggested Robin, so Sun Dance told them about the Swim Man who lived in the sea and came out in the dark, all dripping and foaming, to take people swimming, and about Ningsy who lived in the shed.

"She eats grass," said Sun Dance, "and she's very thin."

"I'm not surprised," remarked Mrs Brogan. "Grass is cheap but not nourishing."

"And she has a cat," said Robin who had heard of Ningsy before, "called Dead Cat. Black."

"Of course," said Mrs Brogan.

"Greenish-black," corrected Sun Dance. "Like oil on the road. Like The Lady's hair."

"Who is The Lady?" asked Mrs Brogan.

"She's another," explained Robin.

"She breathes very quietly down the telephone at me," said Sun Dance.

"Which telephone?" asked Mrs Brogan.

"All the Porridge Hall's telephones," said Sun Dance complacently.

"Porridge Hall is obviously a much more haunted house than I ever imagined," Mrs Brogan observed.

"There's more than that," said Sun Dance. "There's whatever-lives-under-the-stairs, I'm still finding out what it is, and Milko."

"Milko?" asked Mrs Brogan.

"He's the ghost of a milkman," explained Sun

Dance. "He sits on the doorsteps and cries in the night. Into an empty milk bottle."

"How terribly sad!" said Mrs Brogan. "I do hope you're wrong. Are you sure?"

"Quite sure," Sun Dance told her earnestly.

"You make them up!" said Dan. "Admit it!"

"Make them up?" asked Sun Dance, astonished. "How could anyone make anybody up?"

"Well, I don't know where they come from," said Mrs Brogan, "but you'd be an asset to any club, chicken-pox or not!"

"Can I stay the night, then?" asked Sun Dance.

"I'm afraid you can't," said Mrs Brogan. "Sorry, but I'm under orders to send you home in time for tea! I promised I would. Besides, you've got such healthy, strengthening chicken-pox that I'm afraid you will wear out Robin and Dan!"

"I suppose I might," agreed Sun Dance, getting up to go home and cheerfully looking down at Robin and Dan slumped feebly across the sofa. There had been days in the past when he would have loved to find Dan so limp and helpless and he sounded rather regretful as he added, "I could fight Dan easily now!"

"Don't even think of it!" exclaimed Mrs Brogan.

"No," said Sun Dance kindly, "but I could. What would you do if I did?"

"Nothing," Dan told him. "Just lie down and let you kill me."

"Thought so," said Sun Dance, and he went home looking pleased.

"Gone to look for more ghosts," remarked Dan. "I don't know why he doesn't frighten himself."

"Sun Dance's ghosts aren't very ghostly," replied Robin. "He talks about them as if they were ordinary people. Ghosts like his wouldn't frighten anyone."

"Dan," said Mrs Brogan, interrupting and changing the subject, "I think you ought to go and phone your mother. She'll be back from work by now and she's bound to be wondering how you are. She'll be glad to know you're a bit better."

"Am I?" asked Dan.

"Of course you are," said Mrs Brogan. "You're on the mend already and so is Robin. I'll have no malingerers here. Sun Dance is the sort of invalid I like. He's flourishing on his chicken-pox!"

"Tell your mum about Sun Dance's ghosts," suggested Robin.

"Not likely!" said Dan. "She doesn't believe in them and she already thinks Sun Dance is a bit..."

"He's not," protested Robin.

"I know he's not," agreed Dan, "but try telling my mum!"

"It's no good trying to tell Dan's mum anything,"

said Robin, when Dan was out of earshot.

"No," agreed Mrs Brogan. "I do like a person who knows their own mind and Dan's mother is certainly that."

"Do you believe in them?" asked Robin.

"Ghosts?"

"Yes," said Robin.

"Yes," his mother replied, and laughed at his startled face.

"What sort?"

"Sun Dance's sort."

"Swim Man and Ningsy and Dead Cat and The Lady?"

"Not quite," said Mrs Brogan, "but I do believe there are occasionally people who stray from their own time into another."

"What for?" asked Robin.

"I don't know," said his mother to herself as much as to Robin. "Company perhaps. Curiosity. Why would anyone? Why would you?"

"I wouldn't," said Robin, "unless I had friends there."

"Perhaps they have friends there," said Mrs Brogan and she and Robin stared thoughtfully into the fire for a while. When Dan returned a minute later he felt fleetingly and uncomfortably that he had interrupted a private conversation, although he had heard no voices. The feeling only lasted a moment, however. Mrs Brogan's smile was as warm as the fire and Robin's grin was a gleam of welcome.

"How's your mother?" asked Mrs Brogan.

"All right, I think," Dan told her. "She's coming round this evening to have a look at me. And she says Sun Dance can't have proper chicken-pox because nobody has them twice."

"The doctor said they were proper chicken-pox," said Robin.

"I told her that," replied Dan.

"What did she say?"

"She said she expected it was that silly young chap with long hair and the three-legged dog, who'd rather sit and talk than write out a prescription because he never was very bright at school and he only went into medicine because he liked play-acting."

"How on earth did she know that?" demanded Mrs Brogan, laughing.

"She knows a woman who knew his mum," Dan explained.

"Well, I suppose that settles Sun Dance's chicken-pox then," said Mrs Brogan cheerfully, "because as a matter of fact she's quite right. It was that doctor."

"Poor old Sun Dance!" said Robin.

"Sun Dance!" said Dan. "Him and his ghosts and his chicken-pox! Where do you think he gets it all from?"

But nobody knew where Sun Dance found his ghosts, or his stories, or his remarkably convenient chicken-pox. Sun Dance had been puzzling his family and friends for years. They were not convinced by his ghosts and they laughed at his stories and they were often baffled by Sun Dance himself. They would never have believed in his chicken-pox if they hadn't seen the spots.

CHAPTER TWO

In the morning the sun was shining, the sky was clear and the sea was as blue as a midsummer's day, but the wind had a coldness that touched the bone. Autumn had vanished and winter had arrived overnight. There was not a green leaf left in the garden. Sun Dance appeared with the post, glowing with health and chicken-pox and found Robin and Dan still in bed, trying to eat porridge. Robin had decided that chicken-pox felt fairly awful after all. Early in the morning there was very little to choose between being in bed with chicken-pox and being a hobbit in the First Year Christmas play.

"Get up, get up!" said Sun Dance, bouncing on to Dan's bed and then taking a flying leap across to Robin's.

"Mum says we're to stop here until the house warms up," said Robin.

"Oh come outside!" pleaded Sun Dance. "It's lovely outside! Come and play football on the beach!"

"Are you *sure* you're ill?" asked Dan.

Triumphantly Sun Dance pulled up his jumper and shirt and exposed his polka-dot stomach. Dan groaned and pushed his porridge away.

"Can I have it if you don't want it?" asked Sun Dance.

"Didn't you have any breakfast?" asked Robin.

"Only toast and cereal and bacon," said Sun Dance. "I didn't have porridge. Don't you want yours, either?"

Robin shook his head, lay down and closed his eyes, and wondered why chicken-pox should feel so much worse first thing in the morning than at any other time of day. It seemed unfair that Sun Dance should be happily scraping their plates while he and Dan could hardly enjoy orange juice. He thought that Sun Dance was looking far too cheerful to be good company and when his mother came in, she was even worse. She was shining with happiness.

"We've had a letter," she told Robin. "Charley's written!"

"Who?" asked Sun Dance.

"I couldn't believe it when I first saw the name!"

"What name?" asked Robin.

"Charley! After all this time!"

"Who's Charley?" asked Sun Dance. "Who's Charley, Robin?"

"Don't know," said Robin. "Don't care. Feel awful. Ask Mum."

"Where do you feel awful?" asked Mrs Brogan.

"Throat," said Robin.

"Perfectly normal," said Mrs Brogan cheerfully. "Bound to have a bad throat with chicken-pox. And as if you didn't know who

Charley was! It was Uncle Charley all day long from you when you were tiny! He asks if he can come for Christmas!"

"Can he?" asked Sun Dance.

"Of course he can," replied Mrs Brogan. "Say something, Robin!"

"Good," said Robin wearily.

"What *is* the matter?"

"I feel awful," repeated Robin. "Sorry."

"You ate your porridge," said his mother, looking at the empty plates. "You both did."

"We didn't," Dan told her. "Sun Dance had it."

"Sun Dance!" exclaimed Mrs Brogan.

"They didn't care," said Sun Dance.

"Mrs Brogan, do you mind if I stop in bed for a bit?" asked Dan.

"I'm going to," said Robin.

"This is terrible!" exclaimed Mrs Brogan. "You two lying there half-dead, while I feel like singing! Never mind, it's only early-morning chicken-pox feeling. It will pass."

"I feel like singing too," said Sun Dance.

"You'd better come with me, then," said Mrs Brogan, "and we'll leave the invalids in peace and celebrate together in the kitchen!"

"Celebrate what?" asked Robin.

"Oh, everything," said Mrs Brogan. "Come on, Sun Dance!"

"Cracked!" murmured Robin when she had

gone. "Poor old Mum!"

Dan did not reply, because it did not seem polite to agree. From the kitchen came the sound of loud singing and the crash of washing up. The song was "Ten Green Bottles" and there were whoops and cheers every time a green bottle accidentally fell.

"Sun Dance's throat doesn't sound very sore," remarked Dan peevishly. "Do you think they're smashing real bottles?"

"'Course not," replied Robin, and then, after a moment's thought, "They're bashing saucepan lids together, that's all."

"All!" said Dan, in a voice that showed he considered this behaviour heartless in the extreme. "All! Huh!"

Robin understood and quite agreed. It was late in the morning before he and Dan felt well enough to get dressed and join Sun Dance and Mrs Brogan in the kitchen.

"You should have come before," said Sun Dance. "You missed our concert."

"We didn't," said Robin.

"Rude songs and carols," said Mrs Brogan as she poured out mugs of cocoa. "Rude songs by Sun Dance, of course, not me."

"They weren't rude," said Sun Dance.

"Well, they weren't very polite," said Mrs Brogan.

"I know some good ones," said Dan.

"I bet you do," said Mrs Brogan.

"But my throat's too sore for singing," said Dan regretfully.

"It was a concert for Charley," said Sun Dance, "because Mrs Brogan's so pleased he wrote to her. Who *is* Charley? Has he been here before?"

"Oh yes," said Mrs Brogan. "Often! Not recently, though. Not since..." She paused, because the last time Charley had visited had been to come to the funeral of Robin's father. Robin's face, tense and waiting, showed that he was remembering the same event. But he said nothing, and after a moment his mother continued brightly, "Robin, you must remember the summer he spent here when you were six? You howled when he left!"

Dan grinned.

"I don't remember," said Robin. "I'm sure I didn't howl!"

"Oh well," said Mrs Brogan. "You'll just have to make friends all over again, that's all."

"I might not like him," said Robin.

"Of course you will!"

"Is he old?" asked Sun Dance.

"No," said Mrs Brogan. "He's younger than me. He was only a little boy when he first came here. He was nine years old and Nick was eleven and so was I. They stayed with us for a summer while their parents were between houses."

"Between what houses?" asked Sun Dance.

"Between the house they were selling in one part of the country and the house they were buying up here. Charley and Nick came to us so as to still have a proper summer holiday, while all the moving went on."

"Were they brothers, then?" asked Sun Dance.

"That's right," said Mrs Brogan, smiling across at Robin. "Charles and Nicholas. Nick was the naughty one!"

"How naughty?" asked Sun Dance.

"Very," said Mrs Brogan.

"What did he do?" asked Dan.

"What didn't he do!" said Mrs Brogan. "He was always into something. He was a dreadful practical joker, for a start. I shall never, as long as I live, forget the sound of him singing down the dining room chimney!"

"Down the chimney?" asked Dan. "From the roof?"

"Down the chimney from the roof," said Mrs Brogan. "This roof. He nearly gave my mother heart failure and he could have broken his neck!"

"What did he sing?" asked Robin, who had not heard this story before.

"'John Brown's Body', said Mrs Brogan. "It was the gloomiest song he could think of and it came booming down the chimney, like the voice of God, one Sunday afternoon. It ws the most unearthly noise! We had to call the fire brigade to get him down!"

"Was he stuck, then?" asked Dan.

"Stuck?" asked Mrs Brogan. "Not a bit of it! He was standing on tiptoe on the ridge-pole, howling his song into the chimney-pot as if he hadn't a care in the world. Perfectly happy! He was quite prepared to climb down the way he had got up, but my father made him promise not to move an inch until the fire brigade came... Don't you dare look like that, Dan. If I ever hear of you doing such a thing, I'll have you shot!"

"I was only wondering what it was like up there," said Dan. "Nick sounds all right. Was Charley the same?"

"Not at all," replied Mrs Brogan. "Chalk and cheese! Charley was a darling!"

Robin and Dan caught each other's eyes and grinned and Dan mouthed a silent rude opinion of Charley that Mrs Brogan happened to catch.

"He was no sloppy drip!" she said, giving Dan's head a friendly brush. "Far from it! I was the only sloppy drip around that summer. Charley put the rest of us to shame when it came to courage! He was kind-hearted, that's what I meant, always running around after people. He thought Nick and I were wonders. He loved Harriet right from the start..."

She broke off suddenly and changed the subject.

"Lunch! Could you manage soup and ice-cream, do you think? What about you, Sun Dance?"

"Can I have whatever I like?" asked Sun Dance eagerly.

"Depends," answered Mrs Brogan. "What is it?"

"Crisp sandwiches," said Sun Dance. "With cheese inside and brown sauce to dip them into."

"Gosh!" exclaimed Robin in admiration.

"Very funny sort of chicken-pox you've got," remarked Dan. "Me and Robin can hardly swallow!"

"I've got proper chicken-pox all right!" protested Sun Dance indignantly. "I'm much spottier than you!"

"So you are!" said Mrs Brogan. "Take no notice of these two, Sun Dance! You shall have your sandwiches. How many can you eat?"

"As many as you'll give me," replied Sun Dance. "Mum says mine are sympathetic chicken-pox and they've made me terribly hungry. I shouldn't mind soup and ice-cream too!"

"You shall have it," said Mrs Brogan. "Go into the living room, all of you, and you can have it on your knees round the fire. It should have warmed up in there by now. Buzz off out of the way for half an hour and I'll bring it in."

"Who was Harriet?" Sun Dance asked Robin, but Robin did not know and Sun Dance forgot the question when lunch arrived: three plates of soup, three dishes of ice-cream, a large pile of cheese and crisp sandwiches and the brown sauce bottle.

"I don't believe you were ever a sloppy drip!" he told Mrs Brogan, with his mouth full.

"Cupboard love!" said Mrs Brogan.

"You're not one now, anyway," said Sun Dance.

"Mum," said Robin, suddenly remembering Sun Dance's question, "who was Harriet that Charley liked?"

"Harriet?" asked Mrs Brogan. "Oh, Harriet was a long time ago, bless her!"

"The summer that Nick and Charley were here?" asked Sun Dance.

"That's right," said Mrs Brogan, and said no more, as if there was nothing else to say.

"Why did Charley like her so much?" asked Robin.

"Drink your soup," said Mrs Brogan, "and take no notice of your old mother's drivelling! Charley liked everyone!"

"You said Charley loved Harriet right from the start," remarked Sun Dance.

"I talk a lot of rubbish," said Mrs Brogan. "It's old age! It's something you can't understand until you have it, like sympathetic chicken-pox!"

"How old are you?" asked Sun Dance.

"Thirty-eight," said Mrs Brogan mournfully.

"Even older than my mum!" exclaimed Sun Dance, round-eyed.

"How old was Harriet?" asked Robin.

"Eleven," said Mrs Brogan reluctantly. "Harriet and Nick and I were all eleven together that summer."

"In those days," said Sun Dance, "were there cars?"

"Yes, thank you," said Mrs Brogan stiffly.

"Computers?" asked Dan wickedly.

"We didn't need computers," replied Mrs Brogan. "We had brains!"

"They invented the wheel," said Robin solemnly. "Give me a sandwich, Sun Dance! I feel much better!"

"Nick and Harriet will be thirty-eight as well, then," said Sun Dance, handing Robin the sandwich that he had just taken a bite from. "And Charley will be thirty-six. All grown-ups."

"Oh Sun Dance!" said Mrs Brogan.

Robin looked anxiously at his mother and relieved to see that she was still smiling.

"What?" asked Sun Dance.

"Nothing," said Mrs Brogan. "Only it sounded strange when you said it. To think of Nick and Charley and me all growing up."

"And Harriet," said Sun Dance.

"I really can't imagine Harriet grown-up. She was so little. Far smaller than Charley, even, although he was two years younger."

"Was Harriet stopping here, too?" asked Robin.

"No," said his mother. "No. We met her on the beach. It seems to me now that we spent all that summer either on the beach or prowling along the cliffs."

"Were you allowed?" asked Dan.

"Well, funnily enough, we were. The cliffs were nothing like as dangerous, of course. They hadn't crumbled as much as they have now but, even so, we were allowed an awful lot of freedom. People didn't seem to worry the way they do today."

"Was there chicken-pox in those days?" asked Sun Dance.

"No," said Robin who was reviving rapidly with food. "Just the Black Death."

"I bet there wasn't sympathetic chicken-pox anyway," said Dan, and he watched rather resentfully as Sun Dance crunched brown sauce-dipped crisps and swallowed them without flinching.

"*Was* there chicken-pox?" asked Sun Dance.

"Yes," said Mrs Brogan. "There was everything, chicken-pox, mumps, measles, which could be horrible. Poor little Harriet had measles."

"When you met her?"

"Oh no," said Mrs Brogan. "Long before we met her."

"Did you and Harriet wear long skirts?" asked Sun Dance.

"Crinolines," said Robin.

"With parasols," said Dan.

"And ten petticoats," said Robin.

"And hats and veils and long black gloves," said Dan.

"*On the beach*?" asked Sun Dance. "What did the boys wear? Did Harriet have a hat and veil and long black gloves, or was it just you?"

"For goodness sake, Sun Dance!" exclaimed Mrs Brogan. "I didn't quite hobble out of the ark! I wore shirts and shorts or trousers, when it was cold, just like the boys."

"And did Harriet, too?" persisted Sun Dance.

"Harriet! Harriet! Harriet!" said Mrs Brogan. "What's so fascinating about Harriet?"

"Everything," said Robin.

"It's the way you don't talk about her," explained Dan.

"I've *been* talking about her," protested Mrs Brogan.

"Talk more," said Sun Dance.

"I've talked for ages. It's your turn now! How is Old Blanket? Has he recovered from the flea powder?"

"He's stopped sneezing so much," said Sun

Dance, "but he still won't go near Mum and he looks much unhappier than he used to. He's missing his fleas; I'm sure he liked them. They were probably company in the night for him but, anyway, Beany thinks they might still come back. We were going to have a funeral but we couldn't find any dead ones, so perhaps they jumped off and went somewhere safe."

"Did you know Beany was saving those fleas for you?" Robin asked his mother.

"No!" said Mrs Brogan. "Good Heavens! How awful! I hope they didn't go somewhere safe!"

"Mum flea-powdered Old Blanket outside," said Sun Dance, "so if they have gone somewhere safe, Beany and I think it's probably on Mum somewhere. But don't tell her if you see them walking about, will you?"

"I wouldn't dream of it," said Mrs Brogan.

"Because we want them back," said Sun Dance. "*Now* tell us about Harriet! Or can't you remember that far back?"

CHAPTER THREE

"It wasn't *that* far back!" said Mrs Brogan.

The tide had turned and was coming in. All the time the sea was breaking a little further inwards. The beach sloped so gently that yards and yards of wet sand were left empty behind each breaking and retreating surge of water.

"Come on, then!" said Nick.

The game was to follow the sea back as far as possible, wait for as long as the nerve held, and then run like mad in front of the next advancing wave. It was made more exciting because the three children were fully dressed. Charley was wet to his knees in five minutes. He was always the first to be soaked, even though it was Nick and Kathy who stood their ground the longest before turning to flee. Kathy could run by far the fastest of the three and Nick jumped like a cat from ridge to ridge of sand, while the foam broke beneath his feet.

("Were you Kathy?" asked Sun Dance.
"I still am Kathy," said Mrs Brogan.)

Nick turned to follow another wave backwards down the beach while Charley hopped around on one leg, trying to roll his wet trousers up to his knees.

"Mum says Nick was born lucky," he remarked to Kathy, who had stayed to help him. "I wish I had been!"

"It's not luck that Nick's got, it's cheek," said Kathy comfortingly, as she knotted the sodden laces of Charley's plimsolls together and draped them round his neck. "There!"

"Thank you," said Charley, pulling them round to inspect the knot and wondering if he would ever manage to undo it again. "Hey, look, Kathy! Someone else is playing our game!"

Kathy gazed along the beach to where Charley was pointing and saw for the first time that another person was racing with the sea. It was a girl, and she must have watched what they were doing and joined their game from a distance. Kathy and Charley noticed that she kept glancing across at Nick and each time deliberately went out a little further and waited a little longer than he did before sprinting back up the beach in front of the surf.

"She's faster than any of us," said Charley. "Even Nick."

But although the girl was quicker, she obviously hadn't the advantage of being born lucky. As Kathy and Charley watched, she caught her foot on a protruding rock and fell flat on her face.

Kathy reached her first, with Nick close behind and Charley, who had started running before the others, arriving last of all. By the time they reached the girl, she was on her feet again. She stood stock-still and stared and stared at Nick and Charley and Kathy as if she had never seen children before.

"Oh," she said.

For a moment, Kathy and Nick and Charley were too busy staring back to reply. She looked like no one they had ever met before. Her faded green dress was so shabby that it might have been something washed up on the tide, her feet were bare and her hair hung in a chestnut tangle of curls down past her shoulders. She was so alarmingly pretty that Kathy felt slightly annoyed and glanced across at Nick to see if he had noticed.

Nick was reassuringly unmoved; it would never have occurred to him to admire anyone who had not first expressed their appreciation of his glorious self, but Charley smiled at the girl in absolute delight, so hard that she could not help smiling back.

"Your poor knee!" exclaimed Kathy, suddenly catching sight of a trickle of blood running down her leg.

The girl looked at Kathy in astonishment, glanced down at her knee, went perfectly white and collapsed at their feet.

"Fainted!" said Nick dispassionately. "Lay her down flat and pour cold water on her. Scoop up some sea in one of Charley's plimsolls. They're soaked anyway."

"I haven't fainted," said the girl, with her eyes tight shut.

"Well, you've gone a jolly funny colour," Nick told her.

"It's the blood," said Kathy, who was busy struggling out of her jersey. "Mum's just the same. Bother! I forgot this jumper had buttons! Find something to cover it up so she can't see it and she'll be all right."

Nick and Charley obediently turned out their pockets, but found nothing more suitable for hiding the blood than one of Charley's wet socks.

"Well, they were clean this morning," said Charley and tied it carefully in place, while Kathy pulled her jersey over the girl's head.

"You'll be cold," protested the girl.

"Kathy's never cold," said Nick. "Her temper keeps her warm! You might as well put it on, because it's no use trying to argue with her..."

"Shut up, Nick," interrupted Kathy.

"Kathy's the bossy one," continued Nick cheerfully. "Charley's the quiet one..."

"Who are you, then?" asked the girl.

"He's Nick and he talks a lot of rubbish," said

Kathy. "Who are you?"

"Harriet," said Harriet.

"Do you live here?" asked Nick. "Or are you on holiday?"

"Sort of," said Harriet. "I'm not at school, anyway."

Kathy grinned understandingly, because she felt much the same way about school herself.

"We're stopping at Porridge Hall for the summer," said Charley. "Me and Nick are, I mean. Kathy lives in Eastcliffe all the time."

"So shall we, when we get the new house," said Nick.

"Bad news for Eastcliffe!" remarked Kathy.

"What is bad news?" asked Harriet, not seeming to understand the joke.

"Nick living here," explained Kathy.

"Oh," Harriet nodded and, after a moment's thought, added, "but they'll have Charley too" as if that, at least, should be some consolation to Eastcliffe.

Charley stared at her in astonishment. Never before had he been considered as compensation for the trials of those who were forced to live with Nick. Kathy collapsed into laughter and after a moment's thunderstruck silence, Nick joined in.

"I bet that's the rudest anyone's ever been to Nick," Kathy told Harriet.

"Course it isn't," said Nick. "You should hear what they say at school! How old are you, Harriet? Six?"

"I'm eleven this summer," said Harriet with dignity.

"When's your birthday?"

"September," said Harriet.

"Well," said Nick, "you're not eleven this summer. You're ten."

"I'm eleven," said Harriet.

"Are you twelve in September, then?"

"No," said Harriet.

"You're ten, then."

"I'm eleven," said Harriet, "and I'm not arguing. This is a lovely jumper."

The jumper that had fitted Kathy comfortably reached nearly to Harriet's knees and certainly did not go well with her shabby dress, but she obviously did not care at all about such details.

"Keep it if you like," offered Kathy, and added her mother's usual remark. "I expect you'll grow into it."

Harriet pushed up about six spare inches of sleeve and looked very doubtful. Kathy mistook her expression and said, "Borrow it, then. Borrow it for as long as you like."

"All right," said Harriet, smiling.

"Borrow my sock, too," offered Charley eagerly. "Borrow both if you want!"

"Harriet doesn't want your mucky socks!" said Nick.

"They *were* clean," said Charley.

"They don't even match. One's blue and one's grey."

"I can't understand my socks," complained Charley."Mum packed me seven pairs to start with, one for each day of the week, I remember her telling me."

"So what?" asked Nick.

"Now I've only got eleven odd ones. I counted this morning."

"What a nut!" said Nick.

"No, he isn't!" exclaimed Kathy and Harriet simultaneously and Harriet grabbed Charley's hand and said, "Come on, I'll show you my special place! Run!"

Charley forgot about his socks and ran.

Harriet's special place was quite a long way down the coast, a small triangle of shore enclosed by two low rocky barriers, splayed out like fingers from the cliffs above. The sand in that place had a different feel, coarse and crunchy, because it was made up, not of stone, but of millions of tiny fragments of shell. At the back of the little beach was a deep hollow under the cliffs. Years and years ago someone had started to enclose the hollow with a wall and part of it was still there.

"Look!" said Harriet proudly, dropping

Charley's hand to point. "That's my cave!"

"A cave?" asked Charley. "A real cave? Nick's always wanted a cave!"

"This cave is *mine*," said Harriet fiercely.

"Can I go in," asked Charley.

"You can go in," said Harriet, "and so can Kathy..." She paused.

"What about me?" asked Nick, grinning down at her.

"I suppose you'd go anyway," said Harriet.

"Oh no I shouldn't," said Nick. "I should sit at the doorway and howl like a dog."

"You wouldn't!" said Harriet.

"I would!"

"Go on, then," said Harriet, so Nick did and he howled so loudly and pathetically that in a matter of seconds he had been invited inside with the rest.

"It's a lovely place," exclaimed Kathy. "I never knew it was here!"

"You ought to have found it yourself," said Nick reprovingly. "You've lived here for years! Why didn't you?"

"I never used to be allowed to go very far along the beach on my own, until you and Charley came," explained Kathy.

"What are me and Charley supposed to do?" demanded Nick. "Rescue you from dragons?"

Harriet laughed aloud and Kathy replied coldly

that she would like nothing better than to meet dragons and that all Nick and Charley were expected to do was to inform her parents if she were to be swept out to sea and drowned.

"To save them wondering where I was," explained Kathy.

"What a lovely job," remarked Nick. "I can just see me saying to your dad, 'You needn't bother wondering where Kathy is, because she's been swept out to sea and drowned'!"

"I do what I like and nobody minds," said Harriet vainly.

"If I could do what I liked, I would live here in this cave," said Charley. "It's dry as dry and plenty big enough. You could keep all sorts of things in here."

Harriet's guests looked around, half expecting to see all sorts of things stored away already, but the cave was empty of everything but sand and sea shells and it occurred to Kathy that perhaps Harriet had nothing much to keep.

"It would be a brilliant place for storing treasure," she said kindly, and watched Harriet's face begin to glow.

"Treasure!" said Nick contemptuously.

"I've got a book called *Treasures of the Sea Shore*," remarked Charley. "It's full of things you might find. Shells and sea urchins and fossils and stuff like that."

"Pretty soppy treasure!" said Nick. "What I call treasure is gold coins and nothing else and you won't find them here. It's not that sort of beach."

"It's a perfect beach," said Harriet defensively. "You might find anything here. Or I might. You wouldn't."

"Gold coins?" asked Nick.

"Of course," said Harriet with dignity.

"You could look forever but I bet you'd never find one."

"I would," said Harriet.

"Anyway, just one wouldn't count. One wouldn't be proper treasure."

"How many would be proper treasure?" asked Charley.

Nick frowned thoughtfully and then announced that the minimum amount necessary to count as proper treasure would be ten gold coins, all at once, not one at a time.

"All right," said Harriet.

"Would you spend them?" asked Kathy. "I'd buy a horse to ride along the edge of the sea. I once saw a girl doing that..." She stopped and looked at Harriet, puzzled. "Might it have been you?"

"Me?" asked Harriet.

And Kathy, remembering her apparent poverty, changed the subject and asked, "What would you do with treasure if you found it, Charley?"

"I should keep it to look at," said Charley.

"I'd buy a boat," said Nick, forgetting for a moment that he didn't believe in treasure. "A rowing boat. I've always wanted a boat of my own and this bit of beach could be the harbour."

"I didn't know you could row," said Kathy.

"He can row brilliantly," said Charley, who had often admired Nick's beautiful oarsmanship on the pond in the park. "Nick's a fantastic rower. What are you going to do with your treasure when you find it, Harriet?"

"Nothing," said Harriet. "Well, show it to Nick, of course, to prove I was right. And look at it for a little while..."

"Then what?" asked Kathy.

"Put it back," said Harriet.

The room had been growing greyer and greyer as the early December dusk began to fall. Mrs Brogan, who had been remembering a summer forgotten for more than a quarter of a century, suddenly realised that it was nearly dark. When she had finished her story there was no sound except for the crackle of the fire and the muffled thunder of the sea outside. For a moment she wondered if she had talked the boys to sleep, but when she glanced over to them, she found they were gazing at her with bright, puzzled eyes.

"I should like to see Harriet's special place,"

said Sun Dance. "Why haven't I? Why didn't you show it to me, Robin?"

"I've never seen it," said Robin. "I know where the shelly beach is, but I'm sure there isn't a cave at the back."

"There isn't," agreed Dan. "The cliffs are too crumbly for caves round here."

"There was a cave," said Mrs Brogan. "Well, not a cave exactly. A hollow sort of place."

"It's not there now," said Dan positively. "The sea must have got into it and brought it down."

"Harriet told us that the sea didn't come up that high," remembered Mrs Brogan. "Well, I suppose you must be right but I'm sorry it's gone; we had some happy times there."

"It couldn't have been very safe," said Dan.

"Well, probably not," agreed Mrs Brogan. "We weren't very safety conscious. You and Robin have far more sense, I'm glad to say!"

"And me!" said Sun Dance. "Look how I saved Dan from falling off the cliff last summer!"

"So you did!" said Mrs Brogan immediately. "And stop grinning, you two!" she added to Robin and Dan. "I seem to remember that you distinctly told me that Sun Dance pulled Dan up from half-way down the cliff face. It's no good changing your story now!"

"You never asked us how Sun Dance knew Dan was there though, did you?" asked Robin cheekily.

"Or why he didn't fetch help earlier," added Dan. "Like, three or four hours earlier would have been nice."

"I dare say Sun Dance had his reasons," said Mrs Brogan. "Isn't that right, Sun Dance?"

There was no reply. Sun Dance was gazing dreamily out of the window.

"Sun Dance, wake up!" said Robin.

"Where is Harriet now?" wondered Sun Dance out loud, but he did not seem to expect an answer.

"Weren't you listening to anything we said?" asked Dan.

"I was listening to the sea," said Sun Dance. "It does sound loud."

"High tide and a new moon," said Dan.

Robin and his mother, who had always lived by the sea, understood at once but Dan's explanation meant nothing to Sun Dance, although the words immediately fascinated him.

"High tide and a new moon?" he repeated. They sounded like part of an incantation.

"The tides always rise higher and fall lower when we have a new moon," said Mrs Brogan. "Or a full one."

"How does the sea know about the moon?" asked Sun Dance, amazed.

"The moon pulls the sea," explained Robin, "and it pulls harder at a new moon or a full moon, because the sun is helping."

"Helping the moon pull the sea?" asked Sun Dance.

"Yes."

"Where to?" demanded Sun Dance reasonably.

"It sucks it into a sort of bump," said Dan.

"The moon does?"

"Yes."

Sun Dance thought about this amazing bit of information for a moment and then asked, "What about the fish?"

"I've never thought about the fish," admitted Dan. "I suppose they get pulled up a bit, too."

"Why don't they get pulled out of the sea?"

"They're in the sea," said Dan, getting confused.

"What if they were on the beach?"

"They'd die," said Dan firmly.

"What about whales?" asked Sun Dance, determined to understand this phenomenon.

"S'pose whales get pulled as well," agreed Dan reluctantly.

"*A new moon and a high tide sucks up WHALES*?" said Sun Dance. "Why didn't anyone tell me before?"

"You never asked," said Robin laughing.

"Is it true?" Sun Dance asked Mrs Brogan, and Mrs Brogan told him that it really was more or less true.

"At least," she admitted, "it's definitely true

about the water. I shouldn't like to make any promises about the whales!"

"This is magic," said Sun Dance firmly. "Did Harriet know?"

But Mrs Brogan jumped suddenly to her feet, switched on the lights, closed the curtains and banished Harriet back to her own time. Sun Dance was hurried home for his tea and Robin and Dan, who were getting better by the hour, ate scrambled eggs and asked for more. Later, Dan's father came round and they watched the football all evening with two commentaries, one from the BBC, and another, much more interesting, from Dan's father. What he didn't know about the England team wasn't worth knowing and he explained that he came by his knowledge on account of a friend of his, who was the brother of a chap who knew the bloke who did the hair of half the team.

"Perms and streaks and gels and whatever," explained Dan's father. "Highlights and spikes and sprays and I don't know what! They spend more on their hair than they do on their feet. It's no wonder we've never won anything since nineteen sixty-six!"

"Good grief!" said Mrs Brogan.

"I should hate to see our Dan into all that," said Dan's father, rubbing his son's hair over his eyes. "His mum says he looks like the back-end of an old dog, but it's better than being all done up like a girl!"

"I suppose it is," agreed Mrs Brogan.

"And if he's never captain of England," added Dan's father with a perfectly straight face, "it's his hair I shall blame and in a way I shall be thankful!" He got up to go home. "He's a deep one, our Dan is. He's beyond me already! There's not many lads who feel as rough as he did a day or two ago and still remember to pack their Dad's best brace-and-bit when they go away!"

Dan, who had been peacefully grinning at his father, suddenly jumped and looked very guilty.

"I'll look after it," he promised. "It's just for something me and Robin are going to make."

"What would that be, then? asked Dan's father.

"We'll show you when we've done it."

"If you're planning on using my wood," said Dan's father, "you needn't bother showing me. You can pack your bags and go!"

"We won't use your wood," promised Dan.

"That cart you cobbled together last summer nearly broke my heart," said Dan's father. "I'd had that bit of oak since before you were born! And you forced my saw and bent it!"

"Robin's got a saw," said Dan.

"He won't have a saw much longer if you get at it," said Dan's father. "So be warned, Robin! It's more than I was! Goodnight to you all!"

"Goodnight!" they called back, and Dan shouted, "I'll take care of the drill!"

"Old lad," said Dan's father, "I'll take care of you if you don't!" and drove off.

"Good old Dad!" said Dan, when he had gone. "I wonder if he's got any long screws."

"Bed," said Mrs Brogan firmly, drawing back the curtains for one last look at the night. "Oh listen! Poor little Sun Dance! And he went home so happy!"

All the lights were on next door and the night was full of crying.

CHAPTER FOUR

Although Dan and Robin had been allowed to stay up and watch the football, the Robinson children were not. Their mother said it would be finished far too long after bedtime and added that she thought whoever organised late evening international matches on school-days might show a little more sense.

"Mum!" groaned Perry, at this ignorant and unsporting remark.

"Don't groan at me!" said his mother. "School tomorow, so you're going to bed."

"Dad!" appealed Perry.

"Whatever your mother says," said his father. "Set up that video you forced me to buy and you can get up early and watch it."

"I wish I had a television in my bedroom," said Perry.

"You can have one as soon as you leave home," said his father. "Something to look forward to," he added cryptically.

Perry sighed, but recognised when he was beaten. He gave the subject up and went to find Sun Dance, who was the only member of the family who could be relied on to manage the video.

Sun Dance had been very quiet that evening,

much to his family's surprise. Usually he was a passionate football fan (despite his disconcerting habit of identifying with the ball), yet he had not bothered to join in with the pleas to be allowed to watch the match. Nor had he prowled the darkest corners of the house in search of ghosts, or listened breathlessly to the telephone in the hope of hearing The Lady's whisperings. Instead, he had hugged his knees and thought and thought. High tide and a new moon and the new moon pulls up whales. If whales, then why not Sun Dance? Because the whales were in the sea, surrounded by water, soaking wet. Lucky whales, thought Sun Dance. I should drown. Unless my head was sticking out.

Then Sun Dance's mind made a tremendous leap. It isn't the whales that are pulled, he thought. It's the water they live in. The moon pulls water...

And for the rest of the evening (except when roused to programme the video) Sun Dance sat in a dream.

By half-past ten the whole house was asleep, all except for Sun Dance, who had plans for the night.

High tide and a new moon, he reminded himself, and climbed softly out of bed.

No one was better at moving quietly than Sun Dance. He slipped down the stairs like a shadow and finding the doors locked and the keys taken away crawled out into the garden through the dog's cat flap. There he made his way to Ningsy and Dead Cat's shed, collected two plastic buckets, filled them from the outside tap, dunked his dressing gown in one of them, pulled it icy cold and dripping round his shoulders and stood, soaking, freezing and hopeful, a bucket in each hand, waiting.

After the first numbing minute the cold became more bearable. There was no wind and the new moon, a brief silver curve of light, was hooked in a sky full of stars. The buckets were very heavy.

How long, wondered Sun Dance, before I begin to float?

It was not long. He lowered the buckets on to the frozen grass for a minute to rest his arms and immediately felt the delicious lightness beginning. Tightening his grip on the handles, he fixed his sights on the moon. His mind was whirling with stars and excitement and he could no longer feel his feet on the ground.

He was well on his way when there was a crash and a shriek and something enormous grabbed him from behind.

"Let me go!" screamed Sun Dance. "Let me go! Let me go!"

The grabber took no notice, except to hold him

even tighter. Sun Dance bellowed and kicked and sank his teeth into his captor's arm.

"Let me take him!" said Sun Dance's father and Sun Dance came suddenly back to earth.

He was in the kitchen. All the lights were on. The whole family were awake and clustered around him. His dressing gown and pyjamas were lying in soaking heaps on the floor. He was wrapped in a quilt and his back and feet were being rubbed by his parents. He could not stop shaking and he could not stop crying. The room was filled with noise, hundreds of questions from his brother and sisters, thousands of questions from his mother. Sun Dance's sobs grew louder and louder and Old Blanket awoke in the middle of the uproar and began to bark. Old Blanket had twice slept through burglars and once through the collapse of a chimney. Things were bad when Old Blanket barked.

"Clear this rabble!" bellowed Sun Dance's father above the din. "Bed! Now! Out! Do something with that dog!"

The kitchen miraculously emptied. Old Blanket saw the excitement was over and immediately fell asleep. "Silent night," said Sun Dance's father in the silent room. "Holy night. Whatever were you doing?"

"I was just beginning to float," sobbed Sun Dance.

"To float?"

"To the moon," explained Sun Dance, sniffing.

"*To the moon*?" asked Sun Dance's father, considerably startled.

"Not *right* to the moon," said Sun Dance. "Just up a bit."

"How did you propose to get back?"

"Empty the buckets," said Sun Dance.

Mr Robinson suddenly felt terribly tired. He did not ask any more questions, he just hugged Sun Dance and said, "You might have caught pneumonia."

"New what?" asked Sun Dance.

His mother returned from putting his brother and sisters to bed. She brought hot milk and hot water bottles for Sun Dance and hot whisky for herself and her husband and she said,"Oh, Sun Dance. Oh, Sun Dance. Oh, Sun Dance."

"I would have come back," said Sun Dance.

"Oh, Sun Dance," said his mother. "Oh, when I looked out of that window and saw you standing there!"

"Steady on!" said Mr Robinson. "He's all right now! It's just lucky you woke up when you did! It might have been much worse!"

"He's not over his chicken-pox yet," said Sun Dance's mother. "He might have caught pneumonia!"

"What's new moonier?" asked Sun Dance,

beginnng to feel alarmed.

"Nothing, Sun Dance," said Mr Robinson soothingly and mouthed "Don't frighten him!" to his wife. Sun Dance saw the words and began to be really alarmed, especially when he caught sight of a ring of purple toothmarks on his mother's wrist.

"It doesn't matter," she said, seeing what he was looking at. "Nothing matters. We've got you safe and it's all right! There's nothing to be frightened of!"

They carried him upstairs and tucked him into bed, with hugs and kisses, and for a long time he lay very still and listened to their voices rising and falling in the room next door and knew that he had escaped great danger. It wasn't a safe way of getting to the moon. He'd wondered why nobody had tried it before and now he knew. If his mother had not arrived in time, he might never have got back; worse still, he might have caught new moonier and that, judging by the frightened faces of his mother and father, would have been the end of Sun Dance and his bright ideas. All night he drifted between sleep and wakefulness and every time he woke, he was crying, "New moonier! New moonier!" and his mother was saying, "You're quite safe, Sun Dance! Quite safe! Quite safe!" and he would fall asleep again.

The next morning, the chicken-pox club was back down to two members. Perry, Ant and Beany, pausing in the road on their way to school, had attempted to explain by mime the cause of the night's disturbance.

"They must be practising that hobbit dance they've got to do," said Dan eventually, after some minutes of watching Perry and Ant, with their arms pointed into rocket shapes above their heads, leap skywards to the moon.

"Perhaps," said Robin, without conviction, because he couldn't imagine Perry and Ant voluntarily doing any such thing. "But what's Beany doing?"

Beany was doing the sound effects which mostly consisted of roaring. Both leaping and sound effects stopped abruptly when Mrs Robinson opened the front door and shouted some dreadful threat.

"I know people say Sun Dance is crackers," remarked Dan, "but I think they all are, more or less. That Beany is definitely a nutter. Does she wash your bed and breakfast sign *every* day?"

"Every day," Robin told him. "And polishes it at weekends."

Sun Dance did not appear that morning and Robin and Dan missed him very much. They were both feeling more alive than they had for days; their sore throats had gone and their spots had almost stopped itching. Their mothers had a telephone conference about school but decided against it.

"There's flu going round now," said Mrs Brogan, "and there's a lot of difference between feeling well at home and feeling well in a classroom." Dan's mother agreed and said she didn't suppose they were missing much.

"They seem to spend half their time watching school TV," she said. "They could do that at home."

"So they could," said Mrs Brogan, "and I could make the Christmas cake in peace."

"Why does she want to make the Christmas cake in peace?" wondered Robin.

"Because that Charley's coming?" suggested Dan.

"S'pose so," said Robin gloomily, but Mrs Brogan, when questioned, said, "When have I ever not made a Christmas cake?"

"I've never seen you," said Robin.

"That's because you've always been at school," said Mrs Brogan. "Stop moaning!"

It was a very long morning. Robin and Dan sat through half an hour of shopping in French and a documentary about matchstick production and were rewarded for their patience by a Canadian film about beavers.

"This is terrible!" said Robin, after what

seemed hours of leafless trees and empty water. "At least at school the fuse keeps blowing!"

"Beavers are educational," said Mrs Brogan firmly, when she brought in the cake bowl to scrape.

"This programme is a lot more dam than beaver," said Dan and Mrs Brogan laughed.

"I hope Sun Dance comes round this afternoon," said Robin.

"Don't count on it," said Mrs Brogan. "He sounded very upset last night. I'm afraid all those ghost stories weren't a good idea."

"It was Sun Dance who was telling the ghost stories," pointed out Robin. "You were telling us about Harriet. I dreamed about Harriet."

"Did you?"

"What happened to her?" asked Robin. "Did you quarrel?"

"Of course not," said Mrs Brogan.

"Do you still know her, then?"

"What happened to her in your dream?" asked his mother.

"She ran away."

"You're getting as bad as Sun Dance," said Dan. "You'll be seeing ghosts next!"

"Don't give him ideas!" said Mrs Brogan. "If I pop next door to see how Sun Dance is, will you two be all right? You won't set the house on fire or go into a sudden decline?"

"Tell him to come and see us,": said Dan.

"I will if he's allowed out," promised Mrs Brogan. "I'll see what his mother thinks first."

Sun Dance's mother was in her kitchen, looking very tired. She laughed when Mrs Brogan apologised for allowing Sun Dance's ghost stories and said he was as at home with his ghosts as he was with his own relations and that anyway his tales were nothing to the ones that the twins regularly invented.

Sun Dance himself came bouncing through the door before she could explain the cause of the night's commotion, quite his usual self after a morning's sleep.

"Did the chicken-pox club miss me?" he asked.

"It won't be a chicken-pox club for much longer," said Mrs Brogan. "It's nearly better. How are your own chicken-pox, Sun Dance?"

"Fading," said his mother.

"Still there, though," said Sun Dance, pulling out the neck of his jumper and peering down at his stomach to check. "Can I come chicken-poxing this afternoon, Mrs Brogan?"

"Don't ask me," said Mrs Brogan. "I'm not the boss!"

"Can I, Mum?"

"If Mrs Brogan doesn't mind."

"Of course I don't," said Mrs Brogan cheerfully. "Come after lunch and stay to supper and we'll waylay the twins and Beany on their way home from school and invite them, too."

"Are you sure?" asked Mrs Robinson thankfully.

"Quite sure," said her friend, "and you can go to bed for the afternoon!"

"No pestering Sun Dance with questions," Mrs Brogan warned Robin and Dan, when she got back.

"'Course not," said Robin.

"Was it the ghost stories?" asked Dan.

"His mother says not. I don't know what it was and I think it would be better not to ask."

But there was no need for anyone to ask anything. Even before the ritual exchange of symptoms with which the chicken-pox club customarily greeted each other, Sun Dance was describing the perils of the night. He lost no time in explaining how he had nearly been sucked up to the moon and only rescued in the nick of time by the quick thinking of his mother.

"I bit her," he said regretfully. :"You can still see the mark! I didn't mean to. I didn't know who was grabbing me. Lucky that she did, though. Emptying the buckets wouldn't have been enough."

"What buckets?"

"The moon water buckets."

Dan and Robin glanced at each other in silent confusion.

"They should teach you about it at school," said Sun Dance. "They teach you about not getting run over and not getting kidnapped but they never say anything about the moon. They should tell you about not getting moon-napped."

"Sun Dance," said Dan, "you *couldn't* get sucked up by the moon!"

"You said yesterday I could. You said whales did."

"Whales are in the sea."

"That's what the buckets were for," said Sun Dance triumphantly. "Anyway, I did get sucked up! I'd tell my mum to show you the teethmarks, only she's gone to bed."

Robin and Dan gave up. Sun Dance's logic seemed even more complex than usual that afternoon. All they completely understood was that he was now terribly afraid of the moon. They grasped that the night had been somehow dangerous, but where the buckets and bites came into the story they couldn't imagine. Mrs Brogan decided they had discussed the subject for long enough and distracted them by coming in with three aprons and summoning them to the kitchen to learn to cook.

"Cook what?" asked Dan, warily.

"Pancakes," said Mrs Brogan. "And I like mine well tossed and the twins and Beany are coming to tea after school, so you'd better get practising!"

Pancakes passed the afternoon quickly and happily. Mrs Brogan showed them the Porridge Hall method of pancake making, each pancake being no larger than a small saucer and piled in stacks, with orange juice and golden syrup in between.

"We have them rolled up, with lemon and brown sugar," said Sun Dance.

"We have them folded in half, with apple and cream," said Dan.

"Well, now you know the proper way," said Mrs Brogan, "and there is no better, unless it is maple syrup and cream whipped with brandy and I don't happen to have any cream or maple syrup or brandy to hand!"

She also taught them to toss the pancakes, explaining that it was all a matter of courage and not taking your eyes off the ball.

"Pancake," interrupted Sun Dance.

"Pancake," agreed Mrs Brogan. "Oh, well caught, Dan! A double flip!"

The twins and Beany, waylaid before they burst through their own front door and woke their mother, were impressed and envious.

"We've had a terrible, awful day," said Ant.

"Hobbit rehearsals?" asked Dan, and Ant nodded mournfully.

"They've cancelled the singing dwarf bit," she told Dan, "because in the end there was only one dwarf left without chicken-pox or excuses from their mother, but they've put in extra hobbits to make up for it..."

"Don't talk about it," begged Perry.

"Tell us what we've missed," said Robin. "What did you do for the rest of the day?"

"Nothing," said Perry. "Just sat around. We didn't learn anything."

"You must have," said Mrs Brogan. "Think!"

So Perry sat with his head in his hands and thought and thought. "Nothing," he said at the end of this painful process.

"It isn't just pancakes we've learned," said Dan, with a sideways glance at Mrs Brogan. "It was beavers this morning. Very strange animals. Nearly invisible!"

"And impossible to film," said Robin. "And we did French, too."

"French out of books?"

"French off the telly," said Dan. "It took them half an hour to buy six apples and a loaf of bread at this French market they were at and, all the time, you could see a supermarket just across the road. They could have been in and out in five minutes and not had to speak a word!"

"We watched a load of rubbish about matches," said Perry. "I can't remember anything about it, though."

"We watched that," said Dan. "We were hoping

they'd tell us how to make the stuff they put on the ends, but they didn't."

"Thank God for that," said Mrs Brogan.

"I learned something today," said Beany gravely.

"What?"

"A poem," said Beany, and stood up solemnly to recite:

Mary had a little lamb,
She took it to the vicar's.
It climbed into his knicker drawer
And ate his holey knickers.

"So much for education!" said Mrs Brogan.

"I learned another one as well," said Beany, yawning, "but it's too rude. Have you found out what's living under our stairs yet, Sun Dance?"

"Nothing is," said Sun Dance. "I've looked and looked."

"Move in Ningsy and Dead Cat," suggested Dan.

"I've tried, they won't."

"Swim Man, then?"

"Too squashed," said Sun Dance.

"Milko?"

"No milk."

"The Lady?"

"No phone."

"What's the matter with plain old-fashioned

dark?" asked Mrs Brogan.

"Boring!" said everyone.

It was an enormously cheerful afternoon. Beany was allowed to check the bed and breakfast reservations, a favourite treat. Ever since the previous summer, when she had produced a three-course evening meal for unexpected guests during Mrs Brogan's absence, she had felt tremendously responsible for the business.

"Tell Mrs Brogan about the fleas you were saving for her," suggested Perry wickedly, and Beany obligingly did so, thus allowing Mrs Brogan an opportunity to decline with thanks (and horror) the use of any future occupants of Old Blanket's ears. Perry and Ant, reeling under the influence of too many pancakes and too much laughter, climbed on to the table and did their hobbit dance (to colossal applause).

"Do we have to go home?" asked Sun Dance, when Mrs Robinson finally arrived to collect her family.

"Of course you do," replied his mother. "All good things come to an end and, anyway, Robin and Dan look absolutely shattered!"

"I could sit quiet and not say anything," said Sun Dance. "I wouldn't be a bother."

Mrs Brogan and Mrs Robinson glanced at each other. Sun Dance had pulled aside the curtains and was staring worriedly into the night sky.

"It's clouded over," said his mother. "No stars. No moon."

"Oh," said Sun Dance. "Good."

Even so, Robin and Dan and Mrs Brogan noticed that he kept a tight hold on his mother's hand as they crossed the gardens to go home.

"He's still frightened," said Dan. "Fancy being frightened of the moon! I've never heard anything like it!"

"He says he's going to start warning people when he gets back to school," said Robin. "I hope he doesn't. He'll only get laughed at and he hates that."

"He's begun already," said Dan. "He started with a girl who was in the road when we went out to catch the twins."

"I didn't see anyone," said Robin.

"Neither did I," said Dan. "I wasn't watching Sun Dance. But he told me when he came in."

"What did she say?" asked Robin.

"He didn't tell me that," said Dan.

They were back in the living room, Robin and his mother sharing the sofa and Dan on the hearth-rug comfortably scorching his back. Mrs Brogan looked preoccupied as she stared into the flames, and Robin, wondering if she was worrying about Sun Dance, said, "Perhaps they'll understand at school what he's talking about."

"'Course they won't," said Dan. "Scared of the moon! Have you ever met anyone who was scared of the moon?"

"No," said Robin, "but people used to worship the moon. Perhaps they were scared of it, too."

"Who used to worship the moon?" asked Dan sceptically.

"Olden days people. Didn't they, Mum?"

Mrs Brogan did not reply for a moment, although it was obvious that she had heard the question. She looked from Robin to Dan and Dan to Robin like somebody gradually coming awake.

"Didn't who?" she asked.

"Didn't people used to worship the moon?"

"I expect so," she said vaguely.

"So perhaps they were frightened of it too, like Sun Dance?"

"Yes, perhaps they were."

"And Harriet," said Robin.

"Robin!" exclaimed his mother. "How on earth did you know that?"

"I could see you thinking," said Robin. "Your face looks different when you're thinking about Harriet."

"I'd nearly forgotten her," said Mrs Brogan. "Charley writing suddenly brought it all back to me."

"Brought what back?" asked Robin.

CHAPTER FIVE

"Harriet!"

Nick yelled and waved and Harriet came running up the beach to meet them.

"We've been looking for you for ages," said Kathy.

"All day yesterday," added Charley. "Where were you?"

"I was here," said Harriet.

"We didn't see you."

"*I* didn't see *you*!" said Harriet.

"Were you looking for us?"

"No," said Harriet cheerfully. "What did you want me for?"

"We thought we'd teach you to play cricket," said Nick, displaying an ancient cricket bat that Kathy's father had unearthed for them. "So we could play two-a-side; Kathy and you against me and Charley. Kathy's quite good. Or Kathy and Charley against you and me. Charley hardly ever manages to hit the ball properly."

"I'll be on Charley's side," said Harriet.

"It wouldn't be a fair game at all, then," said Nick.

"I should like to be on Harriet's side," remarked Charley.

"Good," said Harriet. "Me and you will be a team."

"Don't be silly," Nick told them impatiently.

"I'm not arguing," said Harriet.

"Oh all right," said Nick crossly. "But you'd better have Kathy as well. Three on to one isn't very fair, but I expect I shall manage."

"You are the vainest person I've ever met," Harriet told him.

"And you are the stubbornest I've ever met," replied Nick.

"Come on!" ordered Kathy. "Stop arguing! Charley and Harriet against you and me, Nick. We can always swop round later."

"Oh all right then," agreed Nick. "Their runs had better count for double, that is, if they make any runs, and no saying it's not fair when we're half-way through the game."

"We'll hit first," said Harriet.

"Bat," said Nick.

"Bat," repeated Harriet, and held out her hand for the cricket bat.

Nick rolled his eyes up to heaven, passed it over, paced out the pitch, announced that he would bowl, and got rid of the last of his bad temper by hurling the ball at Harriet as hard as he possibly could. Harriet hit it a tremendous whack and it landed in the sea.

"Twelve!" shouted Harriet.

An hour and a half later the game was still in progress and Harriet and Charley were winning by one hundred and twenty-two runs to fourteen. Even allowing for Nick's generous double scoring, it was a tremendous total. Nor had it all been achieved by Harriet. She had explained to Charley that cricket was mainly a matter of courage and never taking your eyes off the ball and he had suddenly blossomed into a cricketer.

"I don't know why I never used to like playing!" he said. "It's a brilliant game! I could play all day!"

"You would melt!" Nick replied. "I'm melting already!" And he collapsed into a pool of water.

"Why have you stopped playing?" Harriet asked him. "What's the matter?"

"Nothing now," said Nick rolling on to his back.

Kathy flopped into the pool beside him and said, "If I have to fetch one more ball out of that horrible soft sand, my legs will drop off."

"Aren't you cold?" asked Charley, regarding Nick and Kathy with concern. "You're getting soaked!"

"Cold!" exclaimed Nick. "I wish it would snow! I'm boiling to bits! Get into another pool, Kathy, you're hotting this one up too much! Where on earth did you learn to play cricket, Harriet?"

"School," said Harriet.

"Where's school?"

"I went to a boarding school near London."

"Boarding school!" exclaimed Kathy, sitting up

in excitement. "Oh Harriet, you lucky thing! I've always wanted to go to boarding school!"

"It's the worst place in the world," said Harriet.

"How can it be!" asked Kathy. "I've read about it in books! Sleeping in dormitories and playing jokes on the teachers..."

"Mistresses," corrected Harriet. "You'd get in trouble if they heard you calling them teachers. And dormitories stink!"

"Stink! What of?"

"People. Shoes. Clothes. Something they clean the floors with at the beginning of term."

"Didn't you play brilliant jokes and have midnight feasts?"

"What do you mean, midnight feasts?"

"Smuggle in food and eat it in the middle of the night?"

"No," said Harriet. "How could anybody do that?"

"Well, they always do in books," said Kathy. "Relations send them hampers or they buy things from shops and sneak them in to share."

"I never heard of anyone whose relations sent them hampers," said Harriet, "and people were hardly ever allowed out to the shops. And, anyway, no one would smuggle in food to share. They'd eat it themselves. I would, anyway."

"Oh, Harriet!" said Charley, distressed. "Did you get hungry? Was it awful?"

"It was awful," answered Harriet, "but there was plenty of food. Horrible school cooking, but plenty of it. Stacks. Piles. Mountains. That wasn't why I didn't like school."

"Why didn't you, then?" asked Kathy.

"Oh, too many rules and too many girls and it was so dull and stuffy and boring. I always wanted to be here when I was there."

"You'll have to go back in September," Nick pointed out.

"I won't," replied Harriet.

"Your parents will make you."

"They won't."

"Perhaps you could come to my school," suggested Kathy.

"I've had enough of school," said Harriet stubbornly. "I'm never going to school anywhere again!"

"You have to," Kathy told her. "It's the law."

"I don't care if it is," said Harriet.

"You can't just do as you like."

"I can," said Harriet.

"Shut up, you two!" ordered Nick. "It's much too hot to argue."

"I'm not arguing," said Harriet, with a look on her face that they were already beginning to recognise as Harriet's not-arguing expression.

"Oh well," said Kathy lazily. "Who cares? It's a waste of summer to talk about school! What shall we do now?"

"Cricket," said Charley.

Nick and Kathy groaned.

"We've worn them out," remarked Harriet. She was lying on her stomach, idly sifting through a patch of pebbles and she said, "Look, I've found a bit of agate!"

"What is agate?" asked Charley. "Treasure?"

"No," said Nick. "Ten gold coins is treasure. Nothing less."

"Agate is very nearly treasure," said Harriet and she showed Charley her stone, translucent and ringed with gold and red and white.

"I've got a little amber cat at home," Charley told her.

"An amber cat would be real treasure," said Harriet.

There was no more cricket that afternoon. Nick, when called upon to decide what they should do next, sleepily suggested that they shut up and lie on their backs and look at the sky. One by one they dozed off and woke to find the tide nearly high and a cold wind blowing. Harriet was gone and they discovered that they were each wearing a crown of sticky black seaweed, studded with cockle shells.

"Bother that kid!" grumbled Nick. "Mine's dried on and stuck!"

"They make a sort of glue out of seaweed," remarked Kathy, laughing at his struggles.

"I thought they made soup," said Charley.

"You're thinking of birds' nests," Kathy told him. "Bird's nest soup! It must be disgusting, all sticks and mud!"

"P'raps they sieve it," suggested Charley, after a moment's thought.

"STOP talking rubbish and come and help me unpick this muck!" ordered Nick. "It's stuck much worse than yours was! Harriet is a pest!"

"It's not Harriet's fault your hair is curly," said Kathy.

"S'not mine either!" replied Nick and yelled as Charley removed his crown by the simple method of yanking hard. A lot of hair came off with it and Nick said, "Wait till I see her in the morning!"

But in the morning there was no Harriet to be found. They searched their patch of beach from end to end, eventually making their way to the cave that was Harriet's special place and were astonished by the disappointment they felt when they found that she was not there. Charley lay on his back, disconsolately gnawing the cricket bat, while Nick and Kathy passed the time squabbling in the back of the cave, where Nick was using his pocket knife to carve his name on the wall.

"It was my idea," said Kathy crossly when

Nick, having accomplished the first three letters of his name, glanced provokingly at her and began an H instead of a K. "Nobody calls you Nicholas! You are a pig!"

"Nicholas Jonathan is my name," remarked Nick. "Shall I do the Jonathan or shall I miss it out..."

"Who cares?" said Kathy.

"If I was a pig I would do it," said Nick.

Kathy did not reply.

"I'm glad I don't sulk," said Nick. "I'd rather be a pig than sulk..."

"I'm thinking," said Kathy.

"Not that I *am* a pig," added Nick.

"I hope Harriet doesn't mind you hacking your name in letters six feet high on the back of her cave," remarked Kathy.

"'Tisn't hers," said Nick.

"It is!" announced Harriet, appearing suddenly from nowhere. "It's mine, I told you before and if you cut yourself I shall be sick!"

"Harriet!" exclaimed Charley. "I didn't see you coming!"

"Hallo," said Kathy. "You're always appearing and disappearing!"

"So are you," said Harriet, looking critically at Nick's handiwork. "Did you like your crowns?"

"We could hardly bear to part with them," Nick told her.

"That O you've done is smaller than the other letters," said Harriet.

"Os are hard," said Nick.

"S will be worse," remarked Harriet. "Kathy will be easy to do. All straight lines."

"If Nick ever finishes with the knife," put in Kathy.

"Kathy's sulking," explained Nick.

"Thinking," said Kathy. "Shut up being so aggravating, Nick! I've had a lovely idea!"

"Spit it out, then!" ordered Nick. "Better out than in! Ouch, my thumb! Don't look, Harriet!"

Harriet turned away hastily, and Kathy hurried to distract her attention.

"I looked out of the window last night after we'd gone to bed and it was a beautiful full moon," she said. "Bright silver. It lit up all the beach. What about if we have a midnight feast by the sea?"

"Oh, brilliant!" exclaimed Charley. "Here, in this cave?"

"It would be a perfect place," said Kathy. "We could sneak out and meet up here..."

"Good old Kathy!" said Nick. "What a brain! Let's do it tonight!"

"Could you come?" Kathy asked Harriet.

Harriet stared at her, looking absolutely appalled.

"If you don't want to walk here on your own,

we could come to your house and meet you," suggested Kathy.

"Here?" asked Harriet. "At night? With a full moon?"

"It wouldn't be a bit dark," Kathy told her.

"It would be no good without you," Charley added.

"You're not afraid of the dark, are you?" asked Nick.

"No," said Harriet.

"Anyway, we could come and meet you," Charley offered. "That would be much better. Where's your house?"

"I'm not coming out in moonlight," said Harriet.

"What?" demanded Nick. "Why not? What's wrong with moonlight?"

"The moon's not safe," said Harriet.

"What do you mean?" asked Kathy.

"People can get caught by the moon," said Harriet. "Caught and trapped and dragged away. I know someone it happened to."

"What absolute tripe!" exclaimed Nick.

"You don't know everything," said Harriet. "You don't know anything! And you can't bowl, either!"

"Harriet," said Kathy. "Thousands of people go out in moonlight. Millions! They don't get caught and trapped and dragged away."

"How do you know they don't?"

"How do you know they do?"

"They do," argued Harriet stubbornly. "Some of them do."

Nothing they could say would convince her otherwise. They argued and cajoled and persuaded until they caught sight of a brightness in her eyes that might have been tears. Then Kathy said, "Let's chuck it," and Charley (most untruthfully) added that he would be frightened, too.

"Yes, forget it," agreed Nick. "Poor old Harriet. Come and do your name. Kathy's finished at last. You can borrow my knife!"

"It's Charley's turn and I'm not poor," said Harriet.

"Of course you're not," answered Nick. "Sorry! Well, come on then, Charley."

Charley took the knife in silence while Kathy remarked, too brightly, "People are frightened of much stupider things than the moon."

Harriet sniffed.

"Come and show me what an agate looks like," said Nick, persuasively.

But Harriet would not be persuaded. Nick being nice was infinitely harder to bear than Nick being aggravating and she knew quite well what they were thinking. They were sorry for her. She was frightened. She was poor. She hadn't given

Kathy her jumper back because she didn't have another one to wear and if she appeared without one they would know that. She sat hunched up and miserable and a horrible uncomfortable silence filled the cave until Charley said, "There!"

Kathy and Nick sighed with relief and got up to admire his carving. It was very bad. He had given up entirely on the R so that it read

CHArLEY

But Nick said, "Jolly good. Harriet's turn."

"Go on, Harriet!" said Charley, holding out the knife. "Then we'll all be together."

Harriet sighed but took the knife and began obediently to hack at the wall.

"Shall I help?" asked Nick.

"No," snapped Harriet.

"I only asked. You're pushing too hard."

"I'm not."

"I just didn't want you to cut yourself."

"Mind your own business," said Harriet.

"It is my business," protested Nick. "It's my knife!"

"Keep it then!" said Harriet.

"He doesn't mind you borrowing it!" said Kathy, but it was too late. Harriet had dropped the knife and marched outside.

"Oh, don't go!" begged Charley, but she was already half-way across the beach.

"Should we go with her?" asked Kathy worriedly.

"She doesn't want us," replied Nick. "Poor little kid!"

Harriet must have heard him because she stopped short, turned, stuck out her tongue and shouted, "I'M NOT A POOR LITTLE KID!" before scrabbling over the rocks and out of sight.

"Harriet and Sun Dance would have got on well!" remarked Dan. "Two of a kind! Moonstruck!"

"It's horrible having people sorry for you," said Robin. "Did Harriet ever come back?"

"Yes," said Mrs Brogan. "We did wonder ourselves if we'd see her again but she was there the next morning, waiting for us."

"Quick! Quick! Kathy!" shouted Harriet. "I've left him tied up and he hates it!" and she began to run along the beach. There was nothing for Kathy to do but follow, along the sands and over the ridge of rocks, to arrive breathless and puzzled at Harriet's cave with Nick and Charley behind her.

"Look what I've got!" said Harriet proudly.

"Good grief!" exclaimed Nick.

"Harriet!" said Kathy, "Where did you...? Whose is it...? Why have you?"

"A horse!" exclaimed Charley. "Just what Kathy wanted!"

Harriet smirked and stroked the neck of the fat grey pony she was holding by the bridle.

"What's he called?" asked Charley.

"Snowy," Harriet told him. "He's for Kathy to ride along the edge of the sea!"

"Oh Harriet!" said Kathy.

"To pay you for borrowing your jumper," explained Harriet.

"Is he yours?" asked Nick.

"I've borrowed him," said Harriet.

"You can't just borrow horses!" protested Nick, laughing.

"Snowy's not a horse," said Harriet. "He's a pony."

"I give up," said Nick. "Remind me never to lend you anything, that's all. I can't bear to think how I might get paid back."

"I couldn't find a saddle," said Harriet, ignoring Nick completely and passing the reins to Kathy.

"Who did you borrow him from?" asked Kathy.

"A friend," said Harriet with dignity. "It's quite all right."

"People used to get hung for horse-stealing," remarked Nick to no one in particular.

"Shut up!" said Harriet and Kathy and Charley all together.

"So what did you do?" asked Dan.

"Rode him," said Mrs Brogan. "Of course!"

CHAPTER SIX

On Thursday morning Sun Dance was sent back to school. He did not approve of this, pointing out that since he was the last member of the chicken-pox club to become ill, it was very unfair that he should be the first to return to normal life.

"Yes, but Dan and Robin were much more poorly than you," explained his mother.

"And it still shows where my chicken-pox were," said Sun Dance, ignoring this unsympathetic explanation and inspecting his stomach with care. "The teacher will only send me home again."

But Mrs Robinson had decided that Sun Dance needed something more than ghosts and space travel to occupy his thoughts and she would not relent. Sun Dance was escorted to school, where his teacher unkindly remarked that he looked the picture of health, and the chicken-pox club was once more back down to two members.

"Well, I never thought Sun Dance looked properly ill, anyway," commented Dan, when he heard the news from Mrs Brogan.

"He had spots," pointed out Robin fairly.

"Yes, but they didn't make him ill," said Dan. "They just made him hungry. What'll we do this morning?"

"Something quiet and educational," ordered Mrs Brogan. "I've got to leave you to take care of yourselves while I go shopping."

"Not more school TV," protested Robin.

"Books," suggested Mrs Brogan. "Games, puzzles, tidy your bedroom, I don't mind what you do, so long as it's safe and warm and doesn't cost anything."

"That doesn't leave much," remarked Dan, but when she had gone he suddenly remembered his father's brace-and-bit still packed in his bag upstairs. They fished it out and inspected it.

"Is making a raft educational?" asked Dan doubtfully. "It won't be very warm in your shed."

"It'll be warm enough if we keep sawing," said Robin. "And woodwork is educational. I used to like it when we did it at achool."

"It was better than rotten sewing," agreed Dan. "It's no good them calling it textiles, we all know what it really is. My dad laughed himself sick when I had to do knitting for homework."

Robin grinned sympathetically, remembering the knitting homework. It was sometimes very useful having a dog. Friday had eaten his, although only after much encouragement from Robin and his mother.

"Are you sure you've got enough wood to build a raft? asked Dan.

"Stacks," said Robin. "All the stuff from when

we pulled down the old summerhouse. It's a bit wormy but it's still quite solid. I thought we'd get it all sorted and sawn and drilled in the shed and take it down to the beach in sections and put it together there. Otherwise it'll be much too heavy."

Dan agreed that this was a good idea, and followed Robin out to the shed.

"I once heard a story about a man who built a boat in his cellar," he remarked, as he wrenched out rusty nails.

"What happened to it?" asked Robin.

"Nothing," replied Dan. "Of course. Shall you tell your mum we're building a raft?"

"I hadn't thought," said Robin. "Why, shouldn't I?"

"Just wondered," said Dan, and added after a moment's consideration, "I shan't tell mine!"

As it turned out, there was no time that day to tell Mrs Brogan anything. The moment she arrived home with the shopping, there was a ring at the doorbell and suddenly she had four bed and breakfast guests for the night.

Robin and Dan, who had heard her car returning and hurried out to help her unload, surveyed the intruders with suspicion.

"Townies," said Dan in the privacy of the kitchen. "Silly grins and brand-new wellingtons! Whoever comes on holiday at this time of the year?"

"Oh, there's always a few," Mrs Brogan

replied, as she hurried between kitchen and bedrooms, carrying sheets and towels and dusters and teabags. "I wish I'd had a bit of warning, though!"

"Tell them we can't have them," suggested Robin.

"Too late," said his mother. "Anyway, one night won't kill us and the money will be useful for Christmas. And they only want somewhere to sleep. They said they'd be out on the beach all afternoon."

"What doing?" asked Dan. "Sun bathing? Paddling?"

"Probably," said Robin. "And then they'll come in moaning that their feet are cold and it doesn't look a bit like the picture they saw on a postcard."

"And asking where the flowers have gone," said Dan.

"And the donkey rides," added Robin.

"Shut up, you two!" said Mrs Brogan laughing.

"Well, what are they doing, then?" asked Robin.

"They didn't tell me, but I notice they've brought metal detectors with them so it isn't hard to guess," replied Mrs Brogan.

"Metal detectors?" asked Robin. "Flipping cheek! It's our beach!"

"It isn't, but I take your point," replied his mother.

"Scavenging townies!" said Dan.

"Rubbish!" said Mrs Brogan.

"Metal detectors are cheating," said Robin.

"You wouldn't say that if you had one," replied Mrs Brogan.

At school Sun Dance was having an unexpectedly good time. He found his class all embarked upon a *Treasure Island* project, his class teacher's antidote to Christmas. Already the classroom walls were decorated with painted sailing ships, palm trees and parrots. Even the reading corner had been turned into a log stockade. Arithmetic was done in gold bars and pieces of eight, unruly pirates were tipped the Black Spot, and, despite the awful weather, the entire class turned out and paced the playground, chalking Xs to mark the sites of hidden treasure. Sun Dance was enchanted and by the end of the afternoon his head was full of the glory of buried gold. As soon as he arrived home, he hurried upstairs to ransack his moneybox. It contained eight pound coins, some pyjama buttons (banked in a time of extreme poverty in order to create an encouraging rattle) and IOUs for several million pounds signed by Perry. Sun Dance replaced the buttons and IOUs, pocketed his eight pounds and descended the stairs in three jumps, one for each flight.

"No wonder all our ceilings are cracked!" complained his mother, appearing from the kitchen at the sound of the crashes. "Where are you going?"

"Beach," said Sun Dance.

"Promise not to go out of sight of the house, then?"

"All right," Sun Dance agreed.

"And don't get cold. And don't stay out long. It will be getting dark soon."

"I shall only be a minute," Sun Dance promised.

"Go on with you, then," said his mother.

Sun Dance ran across the road and down to the beach. When he arrived he turned back to look at the house and saw, as he expected, that his mother was standing on the doorstep. Sun Dance waved cheerfully and she went back inside and a moment later the lights of the living room were switched on and he knew that she was keeping an eye on him.

In the playground at school he had learned how to hide treasure, but there the treasure had only been crosses chalked on the asphalt. A chalked cross was nothing. It would wash away with the rain. It didn't matter if it was found or lost for ever. Only the siting of it had been exciting.

"Pick a place to start!" the teacher had ordered.

Sun Dance had chosen the end of the bike sheds.

"Choose a direction, left or right or straight ahead and count the number of paces you take."

Sun Dance had turned right and counted six paces.

"Stay where you are. Find a landmark and move towards it, counting your steps."

Sun Dance had turned towards the lighted office windows, counted six more paces in that direction and then halted.

"Turn to your right. Take five steps backwards (backwards steps are smaller). Mark your crosses!"

That was how they had hidden their treasure at school.

Sun Dance found a largish, flattish stone on the sand, took six paces to his right, turned to face a distant light flashing from the lighthouse further down the coast, took six more steps in that direction, faced right and took five steps backwards. There, at his feet, he buried his eight pound coins.

"You're back soon!" commented his mother a moment later. "Shut the door!"

"I'm not stopping," said Sun Dance. "I just came in to see if I could do it."

"Do what?" asked his mother, but Sun Dance was gone. A minute later he had paced out his steps and triumphantly rediscovered his money.

"It worked!" he shouted joyfully.

"'Course it did!" said a scornful voice behind him. "You only had to look for where you'd been digging!"

Sun Dance spun round and saw that he had an audience. A familiar face was watching him; it was the girl he had warned about the dangers of the moon.

"Or you might have followed your footprints," said the girl.

"Well, I didn't," said Sun Dance crossly.

"I didn't say you did," argued the girl. "I said you might have."

Sun Dance glared at her, selected another stone and paced out another hiding place, being extremely careful to leave no footprints as he did so. Then he dug a hole, buried his money and smoothed the sand back afterwards. The girl hovered beside him, inspecting his smoothing.

"If it disappears, I shall know who stole it," said Sun Dance, and once more he ran back to the house.

"Door!" shouted his mother.

"I'm going back out again!" called Sun Dance.

This time it took slightly longer to find the hiding place, but, even so, in a very few minutes he announced, "There!" and proudly held up his money.

"All of it?" asked the girl.

"Yes," said Sun Dance. "Eight!"

"Only eight?" she asked, sounding slightly disappointed.

"I've got millions more at home," said Sun Dance boastfully.

"You can't have."

"I have."

"I expect eight is all you've got."

"'Course it isn't."

"Why don't you bury some more, then?"

"I easily could if I wanted," said Sun Dance, forgetting that his millions were all theoretical, nothing more than grubby scraps of paper signed by Perry in red paint to look like blood.

"I bet eight is all you've got," said the girl, so scornfully that Sun Dance went home, begged for his pocket money two days in advance, buried that too, and relocated it almost straight away.

"See!" he said to the girl.

"You don't leave it long enough," she said. "You make it too easy. You could never find it again if you left it there all night."

"I could."

"You couldn't."

"I shall do, then."

"I bet you won't."

"I bet I will," said Sun Dance and then almost changed his mind as he caught sight of Mrs

Brogan's bed and breakfast guests, far in the distance along the beach.

The girl sniffed.

"Sun Dance!" said Mrs Robinson. "If you open that door once more I shall go mad! How can I possibly keep the house warm with you letting in a howling gale every two minutes?"

"I'm not going out again till morning," said Sun Dance.

The next day Mrs Brogan's four unexpected guests ate their breakfast in the dining room while Robin and Dan consumed theirs in the kitchen and watched with deep disapproval as Mrs Brogan hurried in and out with porridge and cream, eggs, bacon, sausages, mushrooms, tea and coffee, and piles of toast.

"Do you have to give them so much?" asked Dan.

"I'm not giving it to them," said Mrs Brogan. "They pay for every bite!"

"Did they find anything yesterday?" asked Robin.

"They haven't said," replied his mother, "but I shouldn't think so, because they're trying somewhere else today. They told me they would be driving further down the coast."

"Good riddance," said Robin.

"I'm sure they're perfectly harmless."

"Depends what they found," pointed out Dan ominously and Robin nodded in agreement. They hung around, getting in the way as the bed and breakfasters packed their car, until Mrs Brogan shooed them back into the house.

"Staring is bad manners!" she told them.

"We only wondered what they'd found," said Robin.

"On our beach," added Dan.

"Nothing," said Mrs Brogan.

"How do you know?" asked Robin.

"Just an intelligent guess," said his mother.

"I wish you'd asked them," said Robin.

It was not long before Mrs Brogan was also wishing that she had asked them. Glancing out of the window, she was astonished to see the entire Robinson family, including Mr Robinson (who should have been at work) and all four children (who should have been at school), pacing the beach, excavating large holes in the sand and attempting to comfort Sun Dance, who stood in the middle of his family, alternately roaring with grief and giving orders. Mrs Brogan, accompanied by Robin and Dan, hurried outside to see what was wrong and was told the sad tale of Sun Dance's buried treasure.

"Apparently some girl or other watched him hide it, so I suppose we shouldn't be surprised," said Mrs Robinson.

"What girl was that?" asked Mrs Brogan.

"A horrid, rotten, thieving, burglaring girl," said Sun Dance.

"You don't know for certain that she took it," said his mother.

"Well," said Mr Robinson dusting damp sand off his knees, "it's obviously gone! I give up! I shall have to go to work and these four can come with me. I'll drop them off at their schools on my way. And if we come across that girl, I shall give her a piece of my mind!"

"You mustn't," said Mrs Brogan, who had been feeling more and more guilty as they spoke. "I hate to tell you this, but I had four people staying last night who spent all yesterday afternoon out on the beach with metal detectors! They didn't come in until after dark."

"Yes, and me and Dan knew right from the start that we shouldn't trust them," said Robin. "As soon as we saw their brand new boots and heard the way they talked."

"How did they talk?" asked Ant.

"Haw haw haw down their noses and they said Porridge Hall was quaint and roughing it was all part of the fun."

"I must say I had my doubts," admitted Mrs Brogan, who had overheard them remark that her precious, cherished garden must once have looked quite nice. "I'm terribly sorry, Sun Dance.

I'll make it up to you."

"We should never have let them stop," said Dan. "We could have done with some of Beany's fleas."

"Old Blanket's fleas," corrected Beany.

"Can't be helped now," said Mr Robinson.

"Of course it can," said Perry. "Let's go and get it off them before they escape!"

"Yes, quick, quick, let's go and surround them," exclaimed Sun Dance.

"I'm afraid they've just driven away," said Mrs Brogan.

CHAPTER SEVEN

That ended the treasure hunting. Mrs Robinson hurried indoors to write notes explaining why all four of her children were late for school, while Mr Robinson calmed Sun Dance, mopped him down and rounded everyone into the car. Mrs Brogan and the chicken-pox club returned to the house discussing the lost treasure.

"I told you so!" said Dan.

"I do feel awful," said Mrs Brogan.

"I expect Sun Dance would have lost his money in the end, anyway," said Robin. "It's impossible to find things in sand, even when you've only just dropped them. I only put my knife down for a minute and I never found it again."

"Oh, Robin!" exclaimed his mother. "You haven't lost your knife! Not the one that was Daddy's?"

"I have," admitted Robin. "I've been looking for it for weeks."

"You didn't tell me."

"I kept hoping I'd find it. I knew exactly where I'd lost it."

"I bet those metal detectors picked it up," said Dan. "I *knew* we should have made them tell us what they found before they left."

"It wouldn't have been very polite," said Mrs Brogan.

"Polite!" said Dan scornfully.

"I never thought of them finding my knife," said Robin.

"Even now, we don't really know that they've found anything," pointed out his mother. "Your knife might still turn up, and so might Sun Dance's money. It wouldn't do any harm if you went out and had a look for it yourselves. Be good for you to get some fresh air after a week stewing over the fire, and you never know your luck!"

Robin and Dan looked extremely unconvinced but just in case she should turn out to be right, they abandoned their plans to continue converting the woodwormy summerhouse into an ocean-going raft. Instead, they borrowed Mrs Brogan's garden rake and spent a tedious but healthy morning combing the sand. They found nothing and at lunchtime gave up the search.

"Anyway," said Dan mysteriously, "I've got something much more important to do this afternoon."

"What?" asked Robin.

"Tell you later," said Dan, making tremendous secret signals behind Mrs Brogan's back. "It's to do with me having to go home tonight."

"Oh," said Robin understandingly and asked no more questions, while his mother became suddenly and tactfully engrossed in the table. All the same, she was not very surprised when, as soon as lunch was over, both boys disappeared into town.

"She deserves a proper thank you present," said Dan.

"You don't have to," Robin told him. "She likes having you here."

"I want to," argued Dan stubbornly. "What does she like?"

"Chocolates," said Robin automatically.

"Mum's got her chocolates," Dan told him.

"Stuff to put in the bath," said Robin.

"Mum's got her that, too," said Dan regretfully.

"Those are the only two presents I can ever think of," said Robin, who presented one or the other to his mother on every necessary occasion, birthdays, Christmas, Mother's Day and Easter, with faithful regularity.

They were the only two presents Dan could think of as well, and for a moment they came to a halt until Robin suggested, "Flowers?"

Dan had never bought flowers for anyone in his life, but, nevertheless, he marched bravely into a florist's shop where he stood surveying the contents with a mixture of embarrassment and horror.

"I'm not trailing through town with one of those great soppy bunches," he confided to Robin in a loud whisper. "Someone might see me!"

"What did you have in mind?" asked the

assistnt, sniggering slightly and not even pretending not to have heard.

Dan searched his mind for an unsoppy flower and eventually asked for poppies.

"I'm afraid we don't keep poppies," said the assistant, causing Dan to sigh with relief and leave the shop. Outside the greengrocer's he was suddenly inspired and, without consulting Robin, rushed inside and reappeared a moment later, having purchased a large and prickly Christmas tree growing in a pot.

"What about that?" asked Dan proudly. "Nobody could call that soppy!"

Robin agreed and said it was fantastic, and if he thought privately on the long and back-breaking journey home that his mother could have put up with two boxes of chocolates and saved a lot of trouble, he did not say so. They arrived at Porridge Hall, hid Dan's present in the shed and went into the house to find Sun Dance was back from school and had come round to complain.

"I wish you hadn't gone and had four burglars to stay," he said crossly to Mrs Brogan.

"I wish you hadn't gone and buried your money on the beach and expected it to be safe," replied Mrs Brogan, retaliating with spirit.

"I wouldn't have done if I'd known you were going to start looking after burglars," said Sun Dance.

"They weren't burglars," protested Mrs Brogan.

"They took my money."

"They might not have done and even if they did, they didn't know it was yours. I expect they just thought of it as treasure-hunting. Everyone goes treasure-hunting sometime or other. You've done it yourself and so have I."

"When?" asked Sun Dance suspiciously. "Last night?"

"No, not last night," said Mrs Brogan, laughing. "I can't remember when I last went treasure-hunting. Years ago!"

"Years ago?" asked Sun Dance, suddenly abandoning the burglars and beginning to sparkle. "When you were Kathy? With Harriet?"

"What made you suddenly remember about Harriet?"

"I never forget about Harriet," said Sun Dance. "I never forget about anything! Did Harriet ever find any treasure?"

Mrs Brogan, very glad to leave the subject of burglars, nodded her head.

"Yes?" said Sun Dance astonished, and Robin asked, "What sort of treasure was it?"

"Did Nick count it as treasure?" asked Dan.

"Yes," said Mrs Brogan. "He had to because it was ten gold coins."

At Porridge Hall, back in the time when (as Sun Dance put it) Mrs Brogan was Kathy, it had rained all day. It was not the sort of rain that it is possible to go out in and endure, if not enjoy. It was cold, solid, drenching rain. Kathy's father said cheerfully, when he came home from work that evening, that it was proper Yorkshire summer weather and Kathy's mother replied that it was all very well for him, he had been out all day and not stuck in the house with three irresponsible, misbehaving demons.

"You can't mean my friend Charley?" asked Kathy's father, winking at Charley.

"Well, perhaps not Charley," agreed Kathy's mother. "Charley's been no trouble. He never is."

"And Kathy here has known a few wet days and we've all survived," continued her father.

"Kathy's been no worse than usual," admitted his wife.

"Ah!" said Kathy's father and looked thoughtfully at Nick.

Nick gazed back at him with wide, grey, innocent eyes and said that he had only been practising his bowling.

"Very laudable," remarked Kathy's father.

"Indoors!" said his wife.

"Well," said Kathy's father, "let's have it from the horse's mouth! Or should I say donkey's? Come on, Nick! Where in this house did you find a clear enough stretch of empty space to practise your bowling?"

Nick said that first of all he had tried the upstairs landing and then (having chipped the paint off several banisters and nearly killed Charley coming unexpectedly out of the bathroom) had moved up to the attic.

"I didn't know we had an attic," commented Kathy's father.

"The space under the roof," explained Nick.

"It's not floored," said Kathy's father ominously.

"No," agreed Nick. "It was no good."

Kathy glanced apprehensively at her father. His face and voice showed very plainly how he was trying hard not to lose his temper. He did not ask Nick why the attic had been no good. Instead, he said in a very quiet voice, "Which ceiling?"

"Bathroom," said Kathy's mother. "Cracked right across."

Kathy's father got up and walked out of the room. They heard him climbing upstairs. They heard him come down again and, when he came back into the dining room, his eyes were glinting with anger, but all he said was, "So that was that, eh? No more indoor bowling?"

"I'm very sorry about the crack," said Nick, "but I could easily plaster it up, if you like."

"Don't you dare!" said Kathy's father.

"Then," said Nick, determined to make a clean breast of it, "I tried bowling out of the window."

"Out of the window!" repeated Kathy's father. "Out of which window?"

"Sitting room," said Kathy's mother. "And I could cheerfully have murdered him!"

Once again Kathy's father left his chair and went to inspect the damage. He came back in with his eyes glinting worse than ever and it was quite plain that he no longer cared whether he lost his temper or not.

"I'm terribly sorry," said Nick.

"Dear God, boy!" roared Kathy's father. "Did you never think to open the blasted window first before you hurled your bl...!"

"Peter!" said his wife warningly.

"He did open it," said Charley. "The ball bounced on the rockery outside. That's how the window broke. It wasn't really Nick's fault."

"I'm sure I could put new glass in," added Nick. "I've watched loads of windows being mended at home."

"I bet you have," said Kathy's father. "Well, you've had quite a day and it's going to cost your dad a bob or two in repairs, but I suppose he's used to it."

"And we've had all the lights fuse and the bath drain is blocked," said Kathy's mother.

"I mended the fuse," pointed out Nick

virtuously.

"True," agreed Kathy's mother.

"And I'll unblock the bath as soon as I can get the side panel off. It's only a bit of sand and seaweed in the U-bend."

"His aquarium leaked," explained Charley.

"Nick!" thundered Kathy's father. "Go for a walk!"

"What!" said Nick.

"The rain's nearly stopped. Anyway, I shouldn't care at this moment if you got washed away completely! Go out quickly before I do something I'll regret in the morning!"

"Can we go, too?" asked Kathy, but her father did not reply. He was saying, "One, two, three, four, five, six, seven..."

"Get your coats!" said her mother, while her father continued.

"Eight, nine, ten, eleven, twelve, thirteen, fourteen, I am a patient man, fifteen, sixteen, seventeen, it wasn't my idea to have them here, eighteen, nineteen, the little one is a pleasure to have around..."

The front door slammed.

"Twenty, twenty-one, twenty-two, I'm all right now," said Kathy's father. "Was I too hasty? Perhaps I shouldn't have sent them! It's stopped raining but it's half-dark out there with all this cloud. Shall I fetch them in?"

"Let's have half an hour's peace," said Kathy's mother.

* * *

The beach was grey and uninviting but they went there anyway, half as a sort of penance for Nick's awful deeds, and half in the hope of meeting Harriet. There was no one in sight and they mooched along in a gloomy silence until a pleased "Hallo!" startled them from behind, and there she was, still dressed in Kathy's jumper and her old frock, bouncing up towards them and sparkling with delight.

"Guess what?" she said.

"What?" asked Nick.

"Nothing," said Harriet. "Just a secret I've got. Hallo, Charley! Hallo, Kathy! Can I still borrow your jumper?"

"You know you can," Kathy told her. "I said you could for as long as you liked. Did you get Snowy back all right?"

"Easy as anything," replied Harriet. "Nobody even noticed he had g..."

"I knew you'd taken him without asking!" exclaimed Nick. "I guessed all along!"

"Borrowed," said Harriet.

"Snowy had a lovely time, so why would anyone mind?" asked Charley.

"Of course they wouldn't," agreed Harriet.

"What did you want us to guess?" asked

Charley.

"Something," said Harriet vaguely. "What shall we do?"

"Cricket?" suggested Charley tactlessly.

Nick said cricket was a rotten game and that he had decided to give it up for ever.

"Why?" asked Harriet, but Nick would not reply. Instead he scuffed crossly in the sand while Kathy and Charley related the terrible effect of indoor bowling upon paintwork and ceilings and windows.

"Is he in trouble?" asked Harriet.

"Terrible trouble," Charley told her and Nick said he might go and live in a cave.

"I should like to live in a cave," remarked Charley.

"A cave on my own," growled Nick.

"All right," said Charley peaceably. "Kathy and I will bring you things to eat."

"I shan't," said Kathy. "He can eat winkles and seaweed and serve him right for making Dad so furious."

"And he'd better find a cave of his own," added Harriet. "He's not going to smash mine all up!"

"There's nothing in your cave," said Nick rudely.

"There is!"

"Sand!" said Nick with scorn. "Unless you've stolen any more horses lately."

"How horrible you are!" remarked Harriet with her nose in the air. "I was going to show you something special I found, but I shan't now."

"Oh Harriet!" said Charley.

"I'll show *you*," said Harriet, "and Kathy, but not Nick until he stops being so nasty!"

"Is it here?" asked Charley.

"It's in my cave that Nick said had nothing in it but sand."

"It's much too late to go right up there," protested Nick. "It's nearly dark!"

But neither Kathy nor Charley took any notice of him. They followed Harriet down the beach and into her cave and then there was a great silence until Nick, sulking outside, heard the clink of coins and two loud gasps of delight.

"Treasure!" exclaimed Charley.

"It really is!" whispered Kathy. "Real gold coins! Where ever did you find them?"

It was more than Nick could bear. He charged inside, announcing, "Sorry I was mouldy!" and a moment later had treasure in his hands.

"Ten gold coins!" said Harriet triumphantly.

Nick turned them over and over in amazement. They felt far too solid and well made to be anything but genuine, but still he said uncertainly, "They can't be real gold."

"Bite it," said Charley. "That's what they used to do."

Nick bit one. Nothing happened.

"It should feel soft," said Nick doubtfully, but then Kathy remembered the little gold cross she wore on a chain round her neck and pulled it out for comparison. It was exactly the same colour, and seemed no harder or softer than Harriet's treasure.

"I know my cross is really, truly, gold," said Kathy. "And I've been chewing it every day since I was seven, so I should be able to tell what gold bites like and it's just like Harriet's treasure money. What does the writing round the edges say?"

"Too dark to see," replied Nick, "but there's a queen's head on one side. It doesn't look like our Queen, though."

"There's been piles of queens," said Kathy. "Victoria, Anne Boleyn..."

"The Queen of Sheba," said Charley.

"Queen of Puddings," said Harriet, giggling.

"Harriet!" exclaimed Nick, suddenly coming to his senses. "Where did you get this money?"

"Found it on the beach," replied Harriet.

"Did you dig it up?" asked Charley.

"'Course," said Harriet.

"How did you know where to dig?" demanded Nick.

"Brains," said Harriet cheerfully.

"Brains nothing!" answered Nick. "These are

probably valuable and I bet you pinched them, like you did Snowy!"

"Shut up, Nick!" said Kathy.

"Yes, shut up!" said Harriet. "And I didn't pinch Snowy. I borrowed him! I put him back!"

"Did you borrow these?" asked Nick sternly.

"I might have," said Harriet.

"Don't be so horrible, Nick!" interrupted Kathy. "Of course she didn't!"

"I'm not being horrible," said Nick. "I'm honestly not. I know I was before, but I'm not now, only Harriet borrows too much and she'll get in trouble if she's not careful and I think she ought to put these back."

"You've got a cheek," Kathy told him. "None of the things you smashed today were yours."

"That's different," said Nick, genuinely worried at the thought of lonely little Harriet turning criminal before their eyes.

"It's worse!" said Kathy.

"I think Harriet should put it back," repeated Nick stubbornly.

"She will put it back," said Charley. "She always said she would! It was you who was going to keep it and buy a boat."

"Only if it wasn't someone else's," Nick answered.

"How could you tell if it was someone else's?" demanded Kathy.

"Everything is someone else's," said Harriet.

Nick sighed and said no more. He led the way home, with Kathy glaring furiously at his back and Harriet sniffing and mutinous beside her. Charley deserted them and raced on ahead, but when they reached Porridge Hall and Harriet turned to go her own way, he reappeared and pushed something in her hand.

"It's for you," he told her. "To keep, not to borrow. To do what you like with. It's my little amber cat. You said before an amber cat would be real treasure."

Harriet looked at the little cat. It was much more beautiful than anything she had ever seen. It sat on its haunches and smiled at its thoughts, its tail was a sleek curving wave around its paws and it gleamed with a golden fire.

"Did you really give Harriet your little amber cat?" asked Nick, when he and Charley were in bed that night.

"Yes," said Charley proudly.

"To keep for ever?"

But Charley was not vain enough to expect people to keep his presents for ever.

"To do as she likes with," he replied.

Nick did not ask any more questions, but he reached across in the darkness and rubbed his brother briefly between his shoulder-blades.

"You're a hero all right," said Nick.

"I wish I had an amber cat," said Sun Dance. "What did Harriet do with it?"

"Kept it, I suppose," said Mrs Brogan.

"Who did she get her treasure from?" asked Robin.

"She never would say," his mother told him, "and we let the subject drop. It only upset her."

"Did she give it back?" asked Dan.

"I'm sure she did," said Mrs Brogan. "At any rate, I never saw it again. Come on, Sun Dance! It's nearly dark! Time you were home, and we have to get Dan's things together before his father comes to collect him."

Sun Dance left and Dan began reluctantly collecting his possessions together and squashing them into his bag.

"I wish you didn't have to go," said Robin.

"So do I," agreed Dan, "but Mum says the house is too tidy and they've nearly forgotten what I look like."

"They've seen you nearly every day and anyway, they must have photos," said Robin.

"'Course they have," said Dan. "And it's not as if they even like the way I look. They're always trying to change it!"

"Come on, Dan, cheer up!" said Mrs Brogan. "It would be worse if they didn't want you. Then you would have something to grumble about. Anyway, I expect we'll be seeing you tomorrow morning."

This hope was dashed almost immediately when Dan's father arrived to take him home.

"Son," he said. "Bad news!"

"What?" asked Dan.

"All good things come to an end," said Dan's father solemnly. "Dust thou art and unto dust thou shalt return. Tomorrow is Gran's birthday, as I assume you had forgotten. She's coming to spend the day and Auntie Rose and Uncle Bob are coming too and I am sorry to say they are bringing the twins."

"Oh no!" moaned Dan.

"Well, at least you'll have company!" remarked Dan's father, "and there's howling chaos which is what our house will be tomorrow. The twins are two-and-a-half and the last time they spent a day with us three carpets and the sofa needed shampooing."

Mrs Brogan laughed.

"Still," said Dan's father, picking up his son's bag and climbing into the car, "man is born unto trouble as the sparks fly upwards! And speaking of trouble, I hope you haven't forgotten my brace-and-bit!"

"We need some long screws," said Dan, skilfully ignoring the question. "I was wondering if you had any you didn't want."

"Were you now?" asked his father. "Thanks for

the warning! I shall get a new lock put on my shed door before I'm a day older! Roughly how many were you wondering if I didn't want?"

"As many as possible," answered Robin and Dan together.

"Oh," said Dan's father. "Well. Say goodbye then, Dan, and see you again if I'm spared!"

"Goodbye," said Dan. "'Bye Robin, 'bye Mrs Brogan, I've left you a thank you present in the shed!"

"Oh Dan!" exclaimed Mrs Brogan.

"I hope you like it," said Dan.

"I shall," said Mrs Brogan. "Thank you very much."

The car drove away and Porridge Hall suddenly seemed very large and empty. Robin took a torch out to the shed and managed to drag Dan's thank you present to the back door, so that his mother could inspect it.

"He thought flowers were too soppy," he explained.

"Good old Dan!" said Mrs Brogan. "I shall miss him! What have you two been up to in the shed that requires so many screws?"

"Come and see," said Robin, only too glad to have an excuse not to go back into the empty house for a few more minutes.

"Just for a moment," agreed Mrs Brogan, who quite understood.

CHAPTER EIGHT

"What is it?" asked Mrs Brogan, surveying with interest the remains of her summerhouse, now transformed into a pile of planks, all neatly trimmed and labelled with white chalk numbers.

"Can't you tell?" asked Robin, slightly disappointed.

"Not really," admitted his mother, shining the torch around the shed in search of clues. "A sledge?"

"We never get enough snow for sledges," Robin reminded her.

"True. And it can't be a kennel for Friday because he would never use it, and, anyway, you would never let him. Well, whatever it is, it looks very efficient, all in numbered sections."

"That's so when we put it together the screw holes will be in the right places. It'll make it much easier when we get it down to the beach."

"Down to the beach?" asked his mother.

"It's a raft," said Robin proudly.

"A raft!" repeated his mother. "Good grief, Robin! I must say I'd have given you credit for a bit more sense than that!"

"Mum!" protested Robin.

"I can't believe you've been building a raft!" continued his mother. "Of all the idiots! Well you're *not* building a raft! You're not owning a raft! You're not launching a raft and you're certainly not sailing a raft! And that's that. No arguing."

"All right," said Robin.

"A nice fool I would feel," continued his mother, hustling him out of the shed, locking the door and pocketing the key, "having to ring the coastguard and tell him my eleven-year-old son, brought up all his life within yards of the sea, supposedly of sound mind, has got himself washed out with the tide like some silly holidaymaker!"

"We'll build something else then, if you mind so much," said Robin.

"I know what you're going to say!" continued Mrs Brogan, ignoring him. "You wouldn't go out far! You only want to flat along the coast a bit. You can swim perfectly well. People take rafts right across the Pacific without drowning..."

"Do they?" asked Robin.

"More fool their mothers," said his mother crossly, herding Robin into the house and slamming the door behind him. "What with Sun Dance planning to visit the moon and you and Dan building suicidal rafts, I think having chicken-pox must have addled your brains!"

"We'll make something else instead," said Robin. "We couldn't decide between a raft and a tree-house. Dan wanted a tree-house really, I think. He won't mind."

"I wish you'd stop arguing and listen!" said his mother.

"I am listening," said Robin patiently. "We could build it in that old apple tree that only ever has scabby little apples."

"What on earth have apples to do with anything?"

"You always say they're no good from that tree. They nearly always drop off before they're ripe. It would be a perfect place for a tree-house."

"I'm sorry Robin," said his mother, calming down as suddenly as she had blown up. "What did you say?"

"I said the raft doesn't matter. We'll use the wood to build a tree-house in the scabby apple tree. Dan won't mind. We just wanted to build something. It doesn't really matter what."

"Oh," said Mrs Brogan. "Oh well, sorry then, Robin! I shouldn't have yelled at you like that! But I've watched one home-made raft drift out to sea from this beach and once is enough for me!"

"You never told me about that before."

"You never tried to build a raft before."

"Who was on the raft that drifted out to sea?"

"Who do you think?"

"Harriet?"

"Harriet?" repeated Mrs Brogan, slightly surprised. "No, not Harriet. Harriet wasn't born lucky. Nick was on it. It was his raft," she started laughing. "Poor old Nick! He called it *The Monarch of the Seas!*"

"Where did he get it from?"

"He made it. Harriet helped him. It was just before the end of the holidays, after she had shown us her ten gold coins. It was after the ten gold coins that everything began to change."

"Everything belongs to somebody else," Harriet had said, and although she had always made it perfectly clear that she wanted nobody to feel sorry for her, all the same they could not forget her words and it made a difference.

"Three, three the pipers!" sang Charley. "We are three. Two, two the lily-white boys (that is Nick and me!)"

"Speak for yourself!" snorted Nick.

"Dressed all up in green yo ho! One is one and all alone..."

"Oh, shut up!" interrupted Nick rudely. Recently it had begun to dawn on all of them that Harriet was growing more alone than ever. Charley had noticed and had immediately given her his amber cat; Kathy did nothing as dramatic as that, but always at the back of her mind she had worried about the state of Harriet's clothes and since she could do nothing to improve them, she set about making her own just as bad. In no time at all her trousers were in tatters, her jumpers in lumps, and she had more or less given up brushing her hair. The consequences of this were quite appalling; scruffiness, Kathy discovered, was so time-saving and comfortable that she never completely managed to give it up again and for the rest of her life she was never quite tidy. Also, her gran stopped knitting her jumpers and her mother took her to the hairdresser's where they cut off most of her hair and discovered, too late, that when it was short it grew in natural vertical tufts.

"You look like a frightened clothes peg," said Nick, who had also adopted a policy of extreme tattiness, but got away with it because he was a guest. Soon, of the three, only Charley looked anything like respectable, and even he had lost so many socks and shirts and jumpers since he arrived, that he was down to one set of clothes that grew more and more dilapidated every day. Harriet's faded dress and borrowed jumper soon stopped standing out at all.

"Where do you live, Harriet?" asked Charley one day. "Summerhill," said Harriet. "That house behind the fields at the back of the cliff path."

"I didn't think anyone lived there," remarked Kathy.

"Why not?" asked Harriet.

"It's much too..." began Kathy and broke off

just in time from saying that it was much too tumbled-down to be a home, "too far away," she said, instead.

"Far away from what?" asked Harriet.

"The town, I suppose," said Kathy.

"It's perfect for the beach, though," said Harriet, as if that were all that mattered.

"Can we come and see you there?" asked Charley.

"No," replied Harriet and blushed so red that Charley stared at her in astonishment.

"Charley!" exclaimed Kathy reprovingly.

"Why don't you wait till you're asked?" said Nick.

Nick had almost stopped teasing Harriet. He no longer mentioned her alarming borrowings, often he even defended her, but Harriet had not forgotten his rude remarks about horse stealing and burglars, her name was still unfinished in the cave and she refused to borrow his knife to complete it.

"You said 'Remind me never to lend you anything,'" Harriet told him.

"That was only a joke," replied Nick.

"All right," said Harriet with dignity. "I'll borrow your knife when I start thinking it's funny."

"I just didn't want you turning up again with someone else's horse."

"It was a boat you wanted, not a horse," Harriet reminded him. "I don't know any boats I could borrow."

"Good," said Nick but he did not sound particularly pleased. "It does seem a waste to spend all summer living beside the sea without ever going out on it."

"Couldn't you build a boat?" asked Harriet, but even the optimistic and born lucky Nick had to admit that boat-building was beyond him.

"What about a raft, then?" asked Harriet.

"What a brilliant idea!" exclaimed Nick admiringly, and Harriet blushed again, this time from pleasure.

Kathy was not present at this conversation. She heard about it much later from Nick. Right from the beginning, Kathy was kept out of the raft-building project. In comparison to Nick and Charley, Kathy was quite an expert on nautical matters. This fact caused her to swagger slightly from time to time and annoyed Nick, who did not enjoy being second-best at anything. He persuaded Harriet and Charley that the raft should be a secret, a sort of thank you surprise for Kathy, to be left behind for her private use at the end of the holidays.

"Will she like it?" asked Charley doubtfully.

"Wouldn't you?" asked Nick.

"No," said Charley bluntly. "I'd rather know

what everyone was doing. I should hate to be left out."

"Don't you like surprises?" asked Nick.

"Of course I do."

"Well then," said Nick impatiently. "There wouldn't be any surprises if nobody was left out, now and then."

Harriet and Charley looked at each other and withdrew to discuss the matter.

"Let's ask her," suggested Harriet finally, and the next time she saw Kathy demanded, "What do you like best, Kathy, surprises or knowing before?"

"Surprises," said Kathy instantly.

Nick smirked and Harriet and Charley said, "Oh."

"All right?" asked Nick.

"All right," they agreed.

"Promise?" asked Nick and they both nodded.

"Promise what?" asked Kathy.

"Nothing," said Charley. "It's a secret."

To his dismay Kathy did not react at all correctly. Instead of smiling and looking excited, she got up and marched away. Charley ran after her.

"I thought you liked surprises."

"You're all pigs," said Kathy.

"It's something nice," Charley told her.

"Having secrets without me!" said Kathy

bitterly. "I never thought you would!"

"It's not my secret," said Charley, horribly bothered. "It's Nick and Harriet's really. Harriet thought of it."

This explanation only seemed to make things worse.

"As if I cared about their beastly secrets," exclaimed Kathy.

"I bet Nick would tell you if you asked him."

"I'd rather die," replied Kathy briefly.

"I'll ask him, then," offered Charley.

"Don't you dare!" said Kathy. "Everything's going wrong! Everything! Why has everything changed?"

"Nothing's changed," said Charley. "Well, nothing except perhaps your hair."

"Yes, look at my hair! Awful!"

"I think it looks quite nice," said Charley.

"Oh, Charley!" exclaimed Kathy, completely exasperated.

"Well," said Charley honestly, "I know your hair looks awful chopped off like that, but more of your face shows now. And your face is nice!"

"Charley!" said Kathy and suddenly hugged him tightly. "Promise you won't tell Nick and Harriet?"

"Tell them what?"

"Anything," said Kathy.

"Promise," said Charley.

Nick acquired a hammer and saw ("Borrowed?" asked Harriet, slightly bitterly, and was told there was a great deal of difference between borrowing a rusty old saw and hammer and borrowing a horse.) and bought as many nails as his pocket money would stretch to, and Harriet's cave was turned into a carpenter's shop. The building work progressed very quickly. At first, Nick had thought that the greatest difficulty would be to get hold of enough suitable driftwood, but he had reckoned without Harriet, who had an uncanny ability to find exactly the right piece. There was soon a large heap of flotsam and jetsam piled up outside the cave, including lengths of rope and empty oil cans.

"Have you ever read a book called *Swiss Family Robinson*?" asked Harriet.

"No," said Nick, who was not fond of reading.

"It's about some people who get shipwrecked," said Harriet, undeterred, "and the ship is full of useful things. Food and spades and books and animals. Pigs and goats and dogs and a donkey and they build a raft to take them ashore..."

"Couldn't they have swum?" interrupted Nick.

"Some of them swam," said Harriet. "They swam the pigs and the donkey, with barrels tied to them to make them float..."

"How did they tie a barrel to a donkey?"

"Round its middle. And they tied empty barrels all round their raft as well…"

"They must have had plenty of barrels," commented Nick.

"And I thought oil cans would do just as well," finished Harriet triumphantly.

"Oil cans would be just as hard to tie as a donkey."

"Oil cans for our raft," said Harriet. "Just as well as barrels to make it float."

"We should need an awful lot."

Harriet found an awful lot.

"I could never have found so many," said Nick, "nor so much wood."

"You don't look at the right times," said Harriet.

Charley was very little use as a boat-builder. He was continually deserting the shipyard and running after Kathy, who, at the slightest hint of any secret, took to indulging in furious and spectacular sulks.

"Please let's tell Kathy," begged Harriet, at the end of the second day.

"Girls!" said Nick, whacking in nails at a tremendous rate, while skilfully avoiding his own fingers. "One in a huff and one in a flap!"

"I hope you sink!" said Harriet.

"You'll sink too, then," replied Nick cheerfully.

"I'm not going on it," Harriet told him.

"Her not It," replied Nick.

"Her, then," said Harriet.

"Good," retorted Nick, "all the more for me!"

"Tell Kathy!" pleaded Harriet.

"No," said Nick, "and spoil the secret! Besides, I said I wouldn't."

"Change your mind!"

"I never change my mind," said Nick truthfully. "Anyway, we've nearly finished."

"How are you going to make it steer where you want to go?" asked Harriet.

"Oars," Nick replied, after a moment's surprised thought.

"I'm sure it won't row," said Harriet. "It's too flat and square!"

"Rafts are flat and square!" Nick pointed out. "But perhaps I won't be able to row. I'll find a long pole and push it along like a punt."

"It'll have to be very long, to reach to the bottom of the sea," said Harriet doubtfully.

"It won't be deep, just floating round the coast. People swim out quite far from here."

"What if you get pulled out by the tide?"

"I'll do it when the tide is coming in."

"What if you fall in?"

"I'll swim," said Nick. "Stop fussing! People've been across the Pacific Ocean on rafts."

"Have they?" asked Harriet, surprised. "How many?"

"I don't know," said Nick crossly. "Thousands, I expect!"

"How many drowned?" asked Harriet.

"Harriet!" exclaimed Nick, completely exasperated. "Whose idea was it to build a raft, anyway?"

"Mine," admitted Harriet.

"Well then," said Nick, "stop acting like a girl!"

Harriet, having tried but failed to think of a rude but at the same time unfeminine reply, left him to his hammering and went off to look for a punt pole. It was not an easy thing to find and she searched for a long time before she came across something that she thought might do. Nick found it the next morning, resting against the wall inside the cave and it was so exactly what he needed and yet so like somebody's clothes prop that he had great difficulty in not asking where it had come from.

With the arrival of the pole the raft was complete. It was large and square, a double layer of roughly sawn planks nailed together at right angles to each other and looped around with a necklace of oil can floats. Harriet had strung the cans together by their handles on to a length of knotted rope and Nick had nailed it at intervals all around the edge of the raft.

"It ought to have a name," remarked Harriet. All proper ships have names."

Nick looked fondly at his creation and said he would call it *The Monarch of the Seas*.

"Oh," said Harriet, who had been thinking that the raft might be called after Kathy, which would have been only suitable and fair, or perhaps even after herself, which would have been not only fair, considering the amount of work she had done collecting wood, but also flattering.

"*The Monarch of the Seas*," repeated Nick, who was neither sentimental nor grateful, "and I hope she floats for ever! It's going to be an awful job getting her down to the water. She weighs about a million tons!"

"How will you get off her if she floats for ever?" asked Harriet, watching as he struggled to lift a corner of overweight *Monarch*.

Nick gave a groan of irritation.

"How will you get off if she *doesn't*," persisted Harriet.

"*Harriet*," exclaimed Nick. "Shut up! Stop asking questions! Borrow my knife and go and finish carving your name or something! Anything you like, but stop going on at me! Why don't you do something useful? Why don't you come and help push?"

"Are you going to put her in the water right now?" asked Harriet.

"I'm just going to get her down to the edge. The tide doesn't start coming back in until after eleven, but I want to have her there ready. Then I'll get her afloat and sail her down along the edge of the beach to opposite Porridge Hall. You and Charley look out for me coming and when you see me, run in and find Kathy."

"We've got to get her to the water first," said Harriet, who, having felt the weight of *The Monarch of the Seas*, was beginning to doubt that she would ever really float. After a long spell of hot and breathless tugging, she added, "If we wait until the tide's nearly high, we won't have to carry her so far."

"All right," agreed Nick, who was red-faced and gasping with exertion. "We'll leave her where she is and come back this afternoon. It's not as if anyone could run off with her!"

By four o'clock that afternoon the tide was nearly high and after a short struggle *The Monarch of the Seas* was hauled to the edge of the waves. There she dismayed her designers by sinking slowly to the shingle, so that all that was visible was an un-nautical-looking collection of bobbing oil cans. Nick sighed with disappointment but cheered up a moment later as a larger than usual wave came sweeping in and lifted the raft until she hovered just below the level of the water but definitely afloat.

"Quick! Quick!" Nick shouted to Harriet. "Push her out and pass me the pole!"

Harriet obediently pushed but before Nick

could scramble aboard, *The Monarch of the Seas* was caught by an incoming wave, carried past the launching party, and deposited high and dry upon the shore. Nick and Harriet splashed back after her and tugged her out again and the same thing happened. They launched her six times, each time getting crosser and wetter and at the sixth time Harriet said, "You've made this raft all wrong!"

"I made it just how you said," answered Nick, catching his shins (not for the first time) on the sharp corner of a floating oil can. "It was you who wanted to put these rotten horrible useless stupid cans all around the edge."

"They're the only bits that float," said Harriet. "If you took them off, you'd have to call it *The Monarch of the Bottom of the Seas!*"

Nick stubbed his toe and hopped frantically but did not reply.

"Or *The Rotten Wreck*," said Harriet. "Or *The Soaking Sinker*, or *The Wet Nick*, or..."

"I suppose," said Nick, "you'd have called her *The Lady Harriet*?"

Harriet privately thought that this would have been a perfect name, but replied, "I shouldn't. I'd've called her *The Sniggering P...*"

"She's floating!" interrupted Nick suddenly.
"What?"

"She's floating," repeated Nick. "Look!"

Sure enough, *The Monarch of the Seas* was

rising and falling gently on one spot, not drifting out to sea and not being carried towards the shore.

"Why did she suddenly start floating?" asked Harriet.

"The tide must have stopped coming in."

"Well, hurry up!" said Harriet impatiently. "Get on!"

"Idiot!" said Nick. "The tide's turned! It's going out! I can't go now!"

"You can't go!" exclaimed Harriet. "After all our work!"

"I can't go if the tide's going out," replied Nick, looking ruefully down at *The Monarch of the Seas*. "It wouldn't be safe."

Harriet did not reply for a minute, but stood watching the waves breaking on the shore.

"They're going right up to the same place," she said. "The sea's not going out. It's just staying where it is."

"Is it?" asked Nick, uncertain but terribly tempted.

"I suppose you're scared," said Harriet and knew immediately that that was the one thing she should not have said.

"No!" she said in a panic. "I know you're not scared! Nick, don't!" But it was too late, Nick was already wading back towards the raft.

"Now who's scared?" he asked cheerfully, and clambered aboard.

CHAPTER NINE

Mrs Brogan paused in her story-telling and Friday, who had fallen asleep on Robin's knee, gave a sudden snort and woke himself up for a second.

"Don't stop now!" said Robin.

"It's very late," said his mother. "Aren't you tired? Friday is, poor dog! Look at him!"

"Dogs aren't bothered about ghost stories," said Robin.

There followed a silence that lasted several minutes, while each of them thought their own thoughts. Robin broke it by remarking, "I wonder if dogs ever see them?"

"See what?"

"Ghosts."

"They wouldn't see them, they would smell them," replied his mother. "Smell is their most important sense, not sight. For a dog, a ghost would be an unexplained smell, and for an animal whose hearing was its most important sense, it would be an unexplainable sound. Or an unusual vibration perhaps, for animals like whales. With oilrigs and ships and radar, I suppose the sea is a terribly haunted place for whales these days."

"If there was a ghost that you could see and smell and hear and touch, would it still be a ghost?" asked Robin.

"That would mean we might all be ghosts," said his mother. "How would you tell the difference?"

"We haven't died," said Robin, looking hurriedly away from the photograph of his father that had recently appeared on the mantelpiece.

"How do you know?" asked his mother.

"How do I know?" demanded Robin.

"For all we know, we have died," continued his mother. "I'm sure we wouldn't remember it if we had. We forget being born. I expect we forget dying in just the same way."

"Even if it hurts?" asked Robin, thinking of his father, killed in a car crash more than two years ago, and yet still so alive to Robin that he half expected him to walk through the door at any moment.

"Being born hurts," his mother told him gently, guessing his thoughts.

"Does it?"

"You've forgotten," said his mother.

Robin sprawled in his chair, hugging his dog, warm in a room full of firelight and the sounds of the wind and the sea outside, and he thought, This is happy. This is what it feels like. He grinned across at his mother and asked, "What happened to the raft?"

"Pass me the pole!" ordered Nick. *The Monarch of the Seas* was still hovering in one place, but he had no idea how long this would last.

"The pole?" asked Harriet stupidly.

"The pole for punting!" said Nick. "Kathy's mum's washing line prop!"

"Oh yes," said Harriet, suddenly remembering the clothes prop and handing it over. "What are you going to do now?"

"Float down the coast, like we said. If it starts going out too far I'll jump off. You keep up with me on the shore. Charley promised to keep a look-out for you. He's going to bring Kathy down to the beach as soon as he sees you."

"I wonder what she'll say," said Harriet.

"She'll say we're brilliant and fantastic," replied Nick cheerfully, as he gave a tremendous shove with the pole to start *The Monarch of the Seas* on her voyage. "She'll be impressed. She likes surprises. She'll be really pleased!"

As she splashed her way back to the shore, Hrriet thought that of all Nick's impossible dreams this one of Kathy, surprised, flattering and delighted, was the least likely to come true.

Aboard *The Monarch of the Seas* all was going exactly as Nick had planned. She travelled slowly down the coast, lurching a little from time to time but never enough to dislodge Nick from his proud stance at the helm, always with her garland of oil cans floating and bobbing around her. She stayed so close to the shore, that Harriet's shrieks of alarm whenever Nick looked as if he might fall in, were far too audible. Not many ship's captains are pursued by females begging them to mind the water, they could not put up with it, and neither could Nick.

"Stop squawking!" he ordered Harriet, and when, a moment later, *The Monarch of the Seas* rocked violently and she squawked again, he turned his back to the shore and concentrated on the horizon. It was comfortingly far away and nautical-looking and contained no squealing girls.

By the time *The Monarch of the Seas* had been afloat for half an hour, Nick was in a state of bliss. To be at sea seemed the most perfect thing in the world. He could not imagine how he had managed to spend eleven years on dry land (except for his rowing lessons on the park pond) and he promised himself that he never would again. The only thing that was not working exactly as he planned was the clothes prop. It was not working because he did not need it. He had expected to be punting all the time and if he had not been so fortunate as to be born fearless, as well as lucky, he might have been alarmed at the way *The Monarch of the Seas* had assumed command of the voyage. She was not following her course because Nick was guiding her in that direction, she was following it because she was caught in the current.

Nick did not care. He was spectacularly happy. If *The Monarch of the Seas* had possessed a deck worth strutting, and if it had been possible to take a foot off the planks to do so, he would undoubtedly have strutted. Since he could not do this, he sang instead. Harriet heard the words of "What shall we do with the drunken sailor?" come floating across the water and she wished she had gone aboard.

At Porridge Hall, Charley was becoming more and more anxious. Supper was at six o'clock, sausages and blackberry tart, and Nick had missed it. His sausages were now drying up in the oven and Kathy had eaten his pudding. Nick was devoted to Kathy's mother's blackberry tart and when he first tasted it had earnestly begged her to make it every day. She did not do this, but she made it quite often, usually on the days when she decided Nick was reforming into a better person and she always warned him in advance that it was a blackberry tart day, to ensure that he did not lapse into disgrace during the time that it was in the oven.

"I do hope he's all right," she said worriedly. "He knows what we're having for supper. He's never usually late."

"He's been very busy making a surprise for Kathy," said Charley looking reproachfully at Kathy, who had forced down Nick's helping of tart with great difficulty and was now feeling very uncomfortable.

"Can't say I relish the prospect of any more surprises from Nick," remarked Kathy's father. "I'm sure I've aged ten years this summer! Does he behave like this at home, Charley?"

"Like what?" asked Charley, from which Kathy's father rightly assumed that Nick did.

After supper was over, Kathy went upstairs to lie down and regret her rashness and Charley returned to the beach. Still there was no raft in sight, and no Harriet either, as far as he could see. Evening was coming and the long shadow of the cliffs stretched out across the sand making it difficult to see properly. After a while Charley grew tired of waiting and plodded up the beach in search of the boat-builders.

The current that was carrying *The Monarch of the Seas* followed a long curve, sweeping right in, almost to the shore, before turning and streaming out to sea. Nick and his raft were now on the outward curve. He did not become aware of this until, during a pause between sea shanties, he noticed that Harriet had at last stopped shouting at him. He turned to the shore to signal his approval and that was when he found that the shore was now far away and Harriet nothing more than a little moving silhouette on the sand. Even from so far away, Nick could see that she was waving quite desperately and he was suddenly alarmed. Seizing the clothes prop he prepared to head for the land as quickly as possible. A moment later he discovered that he was in deep water. There was no bottom to push against and the waves clasped the pole and took it from his hands as firmly as if they had possessed it for ever.

Empty-handed and alarmed, he turned to look back at the shore. He had told Harriet that if the raft went out too far he would abandon her and swim. Now, although he was sure that he was too far out, he was much less certain that he could swim the growing stretch of water between himself and the shore. While he hesitated, the distance became wider and wider and it was soon too late to think of swimming.

The sea was choppy this far out. At one particularly violent lurch, Nick sat down and did not stand up again. Clutching the rough planks, he gathered his courage. The tide had only just turned, it would be going out for hours and night was coming, but even so, thought Nick, who was no coward, that was no reason why *The Monarch of the Seas* should sink. Eventually the tide would turn again and he would come back to the shore. Harriet would raise the alarm and people would come and look for him. He knew he was born lucky, and he still hoped it might turn out to be a wonderful adventure. Kathy's mother would save him his blackberry tart. Kathy's father would be terribly angry, and so, too, he supposed, would his parents, but Nick was used to that. Nor was he afraid of what his reception would be at Porridge Hall. Cold and alone on that grey sea, it was very comforting to think of the inevitable hot, bright anger of Kathy's father.

A wave pulled out one of the nails that was holding the string of floats around the raft and an oil can detached itself and bobbed away.

"Kathy!" her mother called up the stairs. "Go after Charley and see where they've got to, will you? I don't like them out on the beach this late."

Kathy got up reluctantly, pulled on a jacket and set off to look for the boys. Five minutes later she caught up with Charley, who was alternately peering along the beach and gazing out to sea.

Mum says it's time you were in," Kathy told him. "What are you looking for?"

"I'm not supposed to tell you till it gets here," said Charley. "I promised Nick."

"Until what gets here?" demanded Kathy.

"I don't know how fast they go," said Charley,

ignoring Kathy's question. "It's taking much longer than I thought."

"What are you talking about?" asked Kathy crossly. "How fast what go? Not another horse?"

"Rafts," said Charley, unhappily.

"Rafts?" asked Kathy. "What rafts?"

"Nick's raft," said Charley.

"Charley!" exclaimed Kathy. "Are you telling me Nick has got a raft?"

"He's been making one with Harriet," confessed Charley. "I thought we ought to tell you and so did Harriet, but Nick wanted to keep it for a surprise. He'll be furious with me for telling you."

Kathy stared at him in horror. "Where is this raft?" she asked.

"Out there," replied Charley, waving his hand vaguely at a hundred miles of ocean. "He's sailing it down this afternoon."

"He couldn't be so stupid!" exclaimed Kathy.

"Harriet was going to come and tell me when he was nearly here, so that I could fetch you."

"Harriet!" repeated Kathy, too shocked for a moment to do more than echo, and suddenly in the distance Harriet appeared. Even in the fading light and from so far away they could see that she was in distress. When she saw them, she waved and waved and pointed to the horizon and Kathy, following the direction of her arm, suddenly saw a small dark shape in the water, far out to sea, appearing and disappearing as the waves rose and fell.

"That can't be him!" she exclaimed. "Look, Charley! Right out there! But it can't be!"

"I can't see anything," said Charley, after peering desperately out at the grey water. "I never can see as well as you. Do you really think it's Nick?"

"It must be," replied Kathy. "Charley! Go and find my dad! Tell him Nick's got a raft and is out at sea and Kathy is watching it from the shore. Go now! And run!"

Charley heard the frantic note in her voice and turned and ran. That was how he was not there when Harriet met Kathy and explained (between sobs) how Nick had taken the raft they had built and gone out to sea on a falling tide ("Becuse I dared him," admitted Harriet in shame), and had ignored her shouts and drifted out further and further ("Singing," said Harriet) until the raft gave a sudden lurch and he disappeared from view.

"So I waited and waited," said Harriet, "because he said he would swim, but he never came... can you still see the raft?"

"Yes," said Kathy, who had not taken her eyes from the sea all the time that Harriet had been speaking.

"Can you see Nick?"

"No. I can just see a bit of black that I think might be the raft."

Harriet sobbed.

"Don't!" said Kathy, reaching out a hand but still not daring to turn aside to hug her.

"I should have stopped him building it," said Harriet, sobbing worse than ever. "I shouldn't have helped. I should have told you. I wish I hadn't said he was scared."

"Dad will telephone the coastguard and he has a friend who keeps a motor boat round at the harbour," said Kathy, trying very hard not to sound furious with Harriet.

"Can you still see the raft?"

"Not now. I thought I did a minute ago."

"Poor Nick," sobbed Harriet. "I'm sure he'll drown. He thought you'd be so pleased."

"If you make me cry, I can't look."

Harriet said no more, but her sobs grew worse than ever; so bad that Kathy had to blink her eyes and rub them and blink again. Harriet saw what she was doing and turned suddenly and fled.

Charley passed her as she ran weeping along the beach and called, "Harriet! Harriet! Come back, Harriet!" but she did not stop.

"Kathy!" panted Charley, arriving breathless at her side. "It's all right! Your dad rang the coastguard and they said they'd send a boat straight away and now he's calling his friend, who he thinks might be nearer and will get here sooner, and your mum's coming as soon as she finds the field-glasses and she said to try and keep your eyes on the place you last saw him. Why did Harriet run away? She was crying."

"She thinks it's her fault."

"It can't be."

"It is, partly," said Kathy, "but it's much more Nick's."

"Don't let's get Harriet into trouble," pleaded Charley, and Kathy nodded in agreement.

A moment later, Kathy's mother arrived with the binoculars and after having focused them where Kathy directed, sighed with relief and offered them to her daughter.

"I saw him quite clearly! I could see him waving!" she told them thankfully. "Kathy! Whatever is the matter? Kathy, darling! Charley! Not you as well!"

Overwhelmed with a mixture of anger and relief, Kathy had collapsed in tears and Charley was not long to follow.

"Stop it, both of you!" commanded Kathy's mother. "Here come the boats! He'll be all right now. At least," she added, suddenly furious herself now that the danger was over, "he'll be all right until I get my hands on him!"

CHAPTER TEN

Nick was safe, tucked up in bed with hugs and hot drinks and now fast asleep. Kathy's father sat beside him, partly in case he woke suddenly and was afraid, but mostly because he did not trust Nick out of his sight. In the morning the boys' parents would be coming to collect them. Kathy's father had telephoned Nick's father and told him that enough was enough.

"We'll always be glad to see him once you get moved into your house up here," he had said, "but I can't be responsible any longer!"

Nick's father said ruefully that he quite understood.

Downstairs, the kitchen was full of people. There was the coastguard (now off duty), the doctor who had arrived to check Nick over, friends and neighbours and Kathy's mother, all drinking tea and talking together. Although it was nearly midnight, nobody had thought to send Kathy and Charley to bed. They hung around, listening to the conversation.

"He's not the first to do it and he won't be the last," remarked the coastguard. "Holiday-makers! Let's hope he learns a bit more sense when he comes to live here! I shall tell him I'm not fishing him out twice! That raft was about gone when we got to him. He must have been born lucky!"

"He was," said Charley.

"Hallo!" said the coastguard, noticing Charley for the first time. "Who are you? One of the boat-builders?"

"Nick's my brother," Charley told him. "I didn't help build the raft, though. Harriet did."

"Harriet?" someone asked.

"Some girl they've been talking about all summer," explained Kathy's mother. "Was she with you, Kathy? Did anyone see that she got safe home?"

Kathy, who in the relief of getting Nick back safely had completely forgotten Harriet, blushed a guilty red and admitted that she did not know.

"She was crying and she ran away," said Charley.

"Poor little soul!" exclaimed someone. "Somebody ought to check she got home all right."

"Where is her home?" asked Kathy's mother.

"Summerhill," said Charley.

"Summerhill? That old ruin?" asked somebody else, amazed.

"Summerhill?" repeated the coastguard. "Harriet from Summerhill?"

Charley nodded.

"And when did you find out about Harriet from Summerhill?" demanded the coastguard.

"What do you mean?" asked Charley. "We've known about her all summer. We've been playing with her. Do you know her, too?"

"I knew Harriet," said the coastguard. "I knew her fifty years ago, when I was a boy..."

"How could you?" asked Kathy, but the coastguard continued, not noticing the question.

"I remember when they told us she'd died of measles at that school they sent her to, as clear as if it was yesterday. And if you've been making a game of her name all summer, I tell you straight, I don't think much of that!"

Kathy and Charley stared at him, speechless, while their world reeled around them.

"Raft-building is mischief and nothing worse," he continued. "That other is meddling and I don't like it and I wish you goodnight."

People were nodding in agreement and looking at Kathy and Charley with something that might almost have been dislike. The coastguard collected himself together and stood up to go home and it seemed to be a signal for the room to begin to empty.

"Oh," said Robin.

"Yes. Oh," agreed his mother, "but you'd guessed, anyway. You guessed a long time ago."

"I remembered the little stone in the churchyard, by the wall," explained Robin. "The one with the sea shells on it. That belongs to a Harriet. But it's very old."

"Nearly eighty years old," replied his mother. "People have always noticed it, because of the sea shells, I suppose."

"What happened next? Did you tell anyone?"

"No," said Mrs Brogan. "And nobody mentioned it again. My father came down and sent us to bed. It had been too much of a day. We were tired out and confused and startled and I don't know what."

"Frightened?" asked Robin.

"Very frightened," said his mother. "At least, I was anyway. We didn't doubt for a moment that our Harriet was the coastguard's Harriet. Charley came tiptoeing into my room that night and said, 'She'll never come back. I know she won't'."

"Good," said Kathy, shakily.

"Poor, poor Harriet," continued Charley. "She was crying. I saw her. She thought Nick would drown and that it was her fault. She doesn't know that he's all right."

"What does it matter now?" asked Kathy, wearily.

"Of course it matters," said Charley. "Where do you think she went?"

"Please don't talk about her," begged Kathy.

"I think she must have gone back to the cave,"

said Charley. "Her special place. I bet she's there now."

"*Don't*," said Kathy. "I'm never going there again."

"She'll be miserable," said Charley, "and she won't have come out to see Nick rescued, even if she could see that far round the coast from the cave. She wouldn't want anyone else to see her. And there was a moon up by then. It's very bright tonight."

He paused, hugging his knees and staring thoughtfully at the moonlit square of window. He was silent for so long that Kathy decided that he had gone to sleep but he roused himself before she could speak and said, "We ought to go and tell her."

"WHAT!" exclaimed Kathy.

"Tell her," repeated Charley, "that Nick's quite safe and all right, so she stops worrying. I can't bear to think of her being sad."

"Charley!" said Kathy, appalled.

"I'm going," said Charley. "I'm going now, before I get scared. Will you come with me?"

"Did you?" asked Robin.

"No," said Mrs Brogan.

"Did he?"

"Yes. He went that night. He slipped out of the house and ran down the beach..."

148

Charley's brave heart failed him at the final barrier of rocks before Harriet's cave. The whole moonlit beach seemed to be silent and listening. Even the sea, once more moving inwards with the tide, made no noise except for a sound like an intake of breath, a small, regular, stifled gasp of regret. Charley had intended to go right up to the cave but he found that he could not. Instead he shouted, "Harriet!"

His voice was louder than the whole, dark, breathing night. It gave him courage.

"It's all right, Harriet!" he called. "Nick's back. He's in bed asleep. He's quite all right."

The silence was even greater than before.

"It wasn't a bit your fault," called Charley, suddenly forgetting his fear in his desire to comfort his friend. "Kathy knows it wasn't. You mustn't worry. Nick's always getting into trouble."

There was no reply. Charley had not expected any. He knew that he would never see or hear Harriet again. She would not return to terrify anyone, especially not somebody who had loved her.

"Harriet!" called Charley for the last time. "Nick was born lucky! You need never worry about Nick! And Kathy will be all right, if Nick's all right. And thank you for teaching me cricket!"

Suddenly Charley was tired. Overwhelmingly, lightheadedly exhausted. The next morning when he told Kathy his story, he could not remember saying goodbye, or climbing down from the rocks, or walking home. He could not remember how he found his own bed but he did find it and clambered in and fell asleep, and awoke in the morning almost perfectly happy.

"And that's why I don't like rafts!" said Mrs Brogan. "And that is a private story for you. Not for Dan or Perry and the rest, and definitely not for Sun Dance!"

"All right," said Robin.

"Promise?"

"Promise. But I don't think they would be scared. I'm sure Sun Dance wouldn't be, anyway. Just think of the Swim Man and Ningsy and Dead Cat and The Lady! And now he knows what's under the stairs as well!"

"What?" asked Mrs Brogan.

"Dark," said Robin. "He says you told him. He calls it The Dark'. He talks to it through the door. 'Dark!' he says, 'I know you're in there!' It sounds awful!"

CHAPTER ELEVEN

There was a cheerfulness spreading through Porridge Hall. It had begun with the letter from Charley that had set off Mrs Brogan's memories of the summer when she and Harriet and Nick had all been eleven years old together. Remembering that time and telling Robin about it had brought Robin's father back into the home again. First Mrs Brogan and then gradually Robin had begun to remember not just that Nick was dead, but also that he had been alive, born lucky, had sung down the chimney, built a raft and drifted out to sea, been rescued (very wet and cold but not noticeably subdued), and had continued in this reckless, cheerful, stubborn, kind-hearted way of life until the terrible day when he had suddenly left it.

"For ever and ever," Robin had supposed, until very recently. Lately he had begun to realise that in real life stories do not end so neatly. Nick's story had become part of his own, and his own was part of all sorts of others, his mother's and Sun Dance's and Dan's, whose father had been Robin's father's best friend.

All linked together, thought Robin. His own links went back and back, back to Harriet who had helped his father build a raft...

"Once is enough!" his mother had said,

referring to Robin's own raft and Robin thought that if Harriet and Nick hadn't built theirs, then his might have been the first. He and Dan might have set sail. Then what? thought Robin.

Dan had not cared what they built. A tree-house was just as good as a raft to him. All he wanted was an excuse to trim planks and drill holes and bang in nails.

"Don't think dad would ever have stood for a raft, anyway," he remarked to Robin.

"I told Mum," said Robin. "She went mad!"

Dan, who was unscrewing an over-tight drill bit with his teeth, could only give an enquiring grunt.

"She said she'd watched one raft drift out to sea and once was enough," Robin told him.

"I know about that," remarked Dan. "My dad told me. He remembered it happening. That's how I knew he'd never stand knowing I was building a raft. This drill has got itself jammed. Pass me the hammer!"

Robin passed him the hammer, Dan gave his father's brace-and-bit a tremendous clout and the jammed part came loose and clattered to the ground in two pieces.

"That's bust it!" said Robin. "What'll your dad say?"

"He won't mind," said Dan. "It's only a drill bit, I'll get him another for Christmas. I was trying to think of something he needed. Did your mum really like that tree?"

"She loved it," replied Robin. "She's keeping it outside until Charley comes and then we're going to bring it in and decorate it."

"Bet that Charley wasn't on the raft with Nick, was he?" asked Dan.

"No," said Robin.

"Too wet!" commented Dan and was slightly surprised when Robin did not immediately agree.

* * *

The day before Charley was due to arrive, the weather changed. For ages and ages it had been icy, either freezing and wet or freezing and dry, but always numbingly, achingly cold. Now, suddenly, the wind changed, the sun came out, and the air became as sweet and warm as spring. Mrs Brogan celebrated by abandoning the housework and taking Friday for a walk instead, and because it was such a brave, cheerful morning she set off in a direction that she had not taken for twenty-seven years.

Which I'm sure Dan would call soft! she thought, pausing for a moment to admire his Christmas tree. Not that I'm certain he ever really believed in the cave anyway, or Robin either, for that matter. And she remembered again their puzzled faces as she had described it to them.

But it can't have disappeared, she told herself. I know Sun Dance thinks I'm ancient, but it wasn't really all that long ago. I can't believe it has gone completely.

It had not gone at all. Mrs Brogan scrambled over the rocks that separated the sandy outer beach from the shelly inside one and immediately saw it, looking exactly as she had remembered it. It was still a special place, solid, secret, bright with morning sunlight and not at all frightening. Friday, who always explored every step of every walk as if it was the first in a new country, dashed recklessly inside and Mrs Brogan followed and there on the wall in front of her was the list of names they had carved.

Nick was highest, enormous, confident letters sprawled across far more than their fair share of smooth rock and slightly squashing Mrs Brogan's own name, which came underneath. It had a distinctly spiky look about it, being all straight lines and chopped out of the wall by Kathy in rather a temper. Beneath Kathy came Charley's scratchy signature and then Harriet, cut carefully and deeply into the rock.

"But Harriet didn't finish hers!" exclaimed Mrs Brogan, stooping to look more closely at the small clear letters. "I'm sure she didn't! She would never let Nick lend her his knife. He offered over and over again!"

("You said, 'Remind me never to lend you anything'!" quoted Harriet.

"That was only a joke," said Nick.

"All right," said Harriet. "I'll borrow it when I

start thinking it's funny.")

"Harriet and her borrowings!" said Mrs Brogan, and then caught sight of something in the corner of the cave and said, "Oh Harriet!" because there, carefully smoothed and folded, lay her old red jumper.

"Oh Harriet, darling!" whispered Mrs Brogan and picked it up and saw there was something small and shining underneath.

Then for a long time she stood between tears and laughter with the jumper and the knife and the ten gold coins clutched in her hands and she thought, Harriet, Harriet, Harriet, and understood how Harriet had managed to produce treasure to show her friends and how she had found enough driftwood to build a raft, not to mention a pony for Kathy to ride, in payment for the loan of her jumper. Harriet had ransacked the years to borrow so much, but in the end it had all been returned.

Outside the cave Friday, who cared for no time but the present, was barking with impatience. When Mrs Brogan came out, blinking, into the sunlight to join him, he ran in circles of delight and then, realising that the expedition had come to an end, took charge of the situation and led the way back home.

Still half in a dream, Mrs Brogan followed him, but before she left the little beach she turned at the top of the ridge of rocks and looked back at the cave to say goodbye. It was not there. In the place where it had been was nothing but tumbled rocks.

So she borrowed that, too! thought Mrs Brogan, well past being surprised by anything else that could happen that morning, and she walked home perfectly happy.

"Where did you get them from?" demanded Sun Dance.

"I found them on the beach," said Mrs Brogan.

"What about those burglars, then?"

"What burglars?"

"The ones Dan said you gave all that breakfast to. Didn't they take my money?"

"No," said Mrs Brogan.

"I know who did, then," said Sun Dance darkly.

Robin said, "My knife! My knife!"

"Where was it?" asked Dan.

"On the beach," said Robin's mother. "And I found Sun Dance's money as well. I expect he'll be wanting you to go Christmas shopping with him tomorrow."

But Mrs Brogan was wrong. Sun Dance had finished his Christmas shopping, ten coconuts (one for each of the inhabitants of Porridge Hall, including dogs) were hidden beneath his bed and he considered these should be more than enough to satisfy anybody. His ten pound coins spent the night under his pillow and the next morning he took them down to the beach and buried them.

"There!" he said, stamping the sand down hard, while Harriet watched. "It's a good job I'm so nice!"

"I only borrowed them," said Harriet, still completely unrepentant.

"Well, you'd better not have come to borrow them again," said Sun Dance, sternly.

"I've come to see somebody," said Harriet, and Sun Dance noticed for the first time that she was gazing intently up at Porridge Hall. As they watched, someone opened a door and came out.

"That's Mrs Brogan," remarked Sun Dance.

"I know," said Harriet. "She used to be Kathy."

"She still is Kathy," Sun Dance told her.

Harriet sniffed scornfully.

"And there's Robin," said Sun Dance. "Nick was his father."

"I know," said Harriet. "He looks just like Nick, only scraggier. Was he born lucky, like Nick?"

"I don't think so," said Sun Dance regretfully. "Except, I've got him a coconut for Christmas. Does that count?"

"What have you got for everyone else?"

"Coconuts," said Sun Dance.

"Doesn't count then," Harriet told him firmly.

"S'pose not," agreed Sun Dance cheerfully.

"Who are those others?" asked Harriet.

"The one up the ladder is Beany," said Sun Dance, watching as Beany, swaying perilously, fastened tinsel and holly to Mrs Brogan's bed and breakfast sign. "And the ones holding the ladder are Perry and Ant. They're wearing their hobbit clothes."

"What are hobbit clothes?"

"Something for a play they were going to do at school but the teacher got chicken-pox and it was cancelled, so they're doing it at home instead. Me and Dan are going to be singing dwarfs and Charley said he'd be a wizard...Look, there's Charley, now!"

Harriet looked and then asked, in disbelief, "Is that Charley?"

"Yes," said Sun Dance.

"Well then, he's got fat," said Harriet. "Much too fat to be a wizard! He never *could* run!"

"Charley's nice!" said Sun Dance defensively. "You should see the presents he's brought!"

"Is that why you like him?"

"Of course not. Everybody likes him. Mrs Brogan said Charley was a darling. Just like me!"

Harriet collapsed into giggles.

"You've got a cheek," said Sun Dance, slightly crossly. "I've been jolly nice about not saying anything about you burglaring my money!"

"Borrowing," said Harriet. "It's awful the way nobody can tell the difference between burglaring and borrowing! I've brought you a present."

"A Christmas present?" asked Sun Dance, slightly alarmed at the thought of having to give her one back and mentally re-counting his coconuts.

"No."

"Good," said Sun Dance, relieved. "What sort of present, then?"

"Shut your eyes and hold out your hands," ordered Harriet. "It's a goodbye present."

Sun Dance obediently closed his eyes and held out his hands and then opened his eyes again to say, "Don't go!"

But it was too late. She had already gone, and Sun Dance was suddenly alone on the beach, and very cold. After a little while he looked down at his goodbye present and found he was holding a little amber cat.

Scraps of conversation floated from Porridge Hall.

"Where did you get it from?"

"Harriet on the beach."

"Harriet is someone Mrs Brogan's been talking about," Dan explained to Sun Dance's family. "A friend of hers from ages ago."

"More of Sun Dance's ghosts," said Perry.

"She was a ghost," said Sun Dance, and everybody laughed.

"Sun Dance found your little amber cat," Robin told

his uncle Charley.

"Good," said Charley.

"He said Harriet gave it to him."

"Perhaps she did in a way," said Charley. "Perhaps she left it for him to find."

"Perhaps," agreed Robin, but he wondered and he remembered an earlier conversation.

"I do believe there are occasionally people who stray from their own time into another."

"What for?"

"I don't know," his mother had replied. "Company perhaps. Curiosity. Why would anyone? Why would you?"

"I wouldn't," Robin remembered saying, "unless I had friends there."

"Sun Dance," said Mrs Brogan. "What did she look like?"

"Who?"

"The girl who gave you the little amber cat."

"Harriet," said Sun Dance.

"How did you know she was Harriet?"

"Of course she was Harriet," said Sun Dance. "She looked like a girl."

"What sort of girl?"

"Any old girl," replied Sun Dance carelessly. "They all look the same to me."

"Sad or happy?"

"Happy," said Sun Dance certainly.